"I've never been a prunes-and-prisms miss, you know."

"I know it well, and am thankful you're not a pattern card of decorum, else you'd never have given me the time of day. And I never cared what they said about me either. Nevertheless, I find that now I care very much that no blame attaches itself to you from my attentions."

"What, not even one step over the line?" She looked down at the rose at her breast. His eyes followed, as she knew they would.

Darius painfully dragged his gaze to her soft, smiling lips and even teeth, her little pink tongue.

"Unprincipled baggage! Not even a smidgen of gossip, so don't tempt me. By Jupiter, if I wasn't determined to do this up proper, do you think I'd be satisfied with two miserly dances? Especially when I know every ramshackle rake in the place will be looking where he's got no business. Let me warn you, my girl, I do not intend to be any complacent . . ."

"Complacent what, my lord . . . ?"

A LOYAL COMPANION

Barbara Metzger

FAWCETT CREST • NEW YORK

A Fawcett Crest Book
Published by Ballantine Books
Copyright © 1992 by Barbara Metzger

Library of Congress Catalog Card Number: 92-97061

ISBN 0-449-22079-6

Manufactured in the United States of America

First Edition: February 1993

To Yang-Sho Sundial Jim,
who is my sunshine

Chapter One

$\int$quire Elvin Randolph was a proud man. He was proud of his vast, well-tended Berkshire acres, and proud of the wealth they brought him, so he and his wanted for nothing. He was proud of the ancient name he bore, and of the sons who would bear it after, and the daughters who graced his fireside. If Squire Randolph had any misgivings, it was that his beloved wife had passed on to an even better life, if such were possible. His chest still swelled, albeit over a comfortable paunch, when he recalled the day Allison Harkness, daughter to the Duke of Atterbury, had chosen him, a simple farmer, to receive her hand and heart. She had never regretted her decision, despite that widow in the village, no, not even when he turned down Atterbury's offer of a title. "A title does not make a better man," she'd said, to his everlasting gratification. He missed his dearest Allison still, despite that widow in the village, but he took comfort knowing she would have shared his pride in the fruits of their union.

The boys were George and Hugh, an heir and a spare as the saying went, solid lads with good bottom. They'd be educated as gentlemen farmers the same as their father: as much book learning as they'd sit still for, with the mud of Randolph's Deer Park Manor only temporarily scrubbed off their hands and faces. There was enough property for Hugh, the second son, to claim a tidy parcel, or enough income to purchase his colors if the little hellion didn't outgrow his love of knights and dragons, pirates and Indians.

The girls would be well provided for, too, their mother's portion making them heiresses in their own rights. Catherine, Squire's firstborn child, had also inherited her mother's delicate beauty. She was soft-spoken and well mannered, even as a tiny moppet in sparkling, starched pinafore and smooth blond braids. A lady to her fine-boned fingers, she was destined to grace London ballrooms, to shine as an ornament of society, to make a noble marriage. Her grandmother, the dowager Duchess of Atterbury, was already planning her come-out, with the squire's blessings. Frankly, Catherine's perfection terrified Randolph. What if he got her dirty, or uttered a profanity in her hearing, or touched her soft skin too hard with his rough hands? Better the dowager saw to such a paragon. He'd look after the boys, and Sonia. . . .

If the dark-haired, sturdy boys were as alike as two cherries on the same vine, the squire's daughters were as similar as apples and oranges. Catherine was refined elegance, with the cool essence of silvery moonlight. Sonia was exuberant sunshine, all bouncy golden curls and bluebell eyes and a dimpled smile that could melt the frostiest heart, which the squire's certainly was not. The baby of the family, younger than Catherine by ten years and soon left motherless besides, Sonia was pampered and spoiled and adored by the whole household.

"You'll ruin that child," the dowager duchess warned. "Letting her run wild after the boys like that, taking her up on your horse with you every time she holds her arms out, instead of sending her back to the nursery where she belongs. Mark my words, Elvin, that gel will be a rare handful. No man will take a hoyden to wife."

"But she's just an infant, Lady Almeria," Squire replied, brushing cookie crumbs from his now-rumpled cravat. "Time enough to worry about a husband later."

The dowager only sniffed. "She doesn't even know the meaning of the word 'no.' "

"Of course she does." Randolph tossed the babe up in the air and asked: "Precious Sunny, do you want a fussy old rich man with a title to take you away and keep you in some cold, dark castle?"

"No," she shouted between squeals. "No, Papa, no!"

Squire called her Sunny, not Sonny with an o. He denied his mother-in-law's claims that he was trying to make another son out of the girl. He was content with his boys, and absolutely delighted with this pink and white bundle that was soft but not fragile like porcelain, sweet but not cloying like wedding cake. Besides, no little boy would be so generous with sticky hugs and sloppy kisses. He called his youngest child Sunny simply because she lit up his life. When she looked up at him with adoration, he saw her mother, Allison, and he was proud all over again.

Unfortunately, when Sonia looked up at him like that, Squire Randolph could deny her nothing. Even more unfortunately, perhaps, Sonia also inherited, beyond Allison Harkness's beauty, fortune, and loving nature, her mother's knack of knowing her own mind. Allison had always known what she wanted, and had accepted nothing less. Didn't she marry plain Elvin Randolph, Esq., despite an uproar that shook stately Atterbury House in Grosvenor Square to its very foundations? So, too, did Miss Sonia Randolph make her wishes known. Poor

Elvin had more than one opportunity to think back on the dowager's dire warnings. Especially when it came to his hounds.

Now, as proud as he might be, Squire Randolph did not take credit for his lands. They were passed down to him, as he'd hand them on to George. That they were fertile was a gift from on high, to be nurtured and tended as best he could. Even his children, as much as he loved them, were more products of Allison's goodness than his own, he felt. But his hounds? Ah, now, there was something a man could brag about to his cronies. He could invite those toffs down from London and show off his darlings till the titles turned green with envy. Hadn't he bred the dogs himself, for generation after generation, to get just the right conformation, just the perfect pitch, color, and temperament? Hadn't he trained them all himself, right from the weaning box, till he had the best fox-hunting pack in the county, maybe the country? By Jupiter, he had!

Sheltonford was not Quorn territory, and the squire was too conscientious to let anyone destroy his tenants' fields or disturb their herds, fox or no, but an invite to ride with the Deer Park pack was seldom refused. When there was no company or no fox, Randolph had one of his kennelmen drag a hide for him, just so the hounds stayed keen, just so he could have the joy of riding behind, a fine piece of horseflesh between his legs, the wind in his face, and the sound of a dog on the scent like music in his ears. Aw-roo! Aw-roo!

Squire could pick out the individual hounds' voices the same as he could identify his children's. Better, for there was Belle, first to find the scent, loudest to bay, sweetest in timbre. Belle was the best dog Squire ever owned. Gold and white, with velvet ears and doe eyes, her tail arched just so, she stood foursquare and jaunty, always eager. Her heart was in the hunt, and Elvin Randolph's heart rode with her.

* * *

Bud Kemp was also a proud man. He ran over
three hundred head of fat and fluffy black-faced
sheep on hundreds of acres of land he leased from
Squire Randolph, just like his father before him,
and he'd never missed a rent day. He had three
strapping boys to help him at lambing, shearing,
and market days, with another gone for a soldier.
The youngest was studying with the vicar to see if
he'd suit the priesthood. His wife still looked good
to him, especially in the dark, and they had enough
money set by in case times got hard. Bud Kemp
could rest easy nights, knowing he'd done right by
his family, his landlord, his church, and his country. He could also sleep soundly knowing his woolly
assets were safe out in the valleys with his dogs,
the smartest, loyalest, most competent sheepdogs
in the shire. Hadn't Bud bred them himself for generations, right since crossing his older border collie
bitch with Shep Hayduck's Belgian herder? Damn
right, he had. And kept breeding the good 'uns back
to the lines to weed out the bullies, the daydream-
ers, and the weak of body or soul.

Those sheep were the stupidest creatures on four
legs. They'd get lost in the front yard if not for the
dogs. They'd panic at the slide of a pebble on a
slope, graze clean off a cliff, or baa in the face of a
long-knifed poacher, if not for the dogs. Bud Kemp's
sheepdogs kept him snoring, and the dog that
brought a smile to his weathered face, even in his
dreams, was Jack.

Jack was a handsome black dog, well-furred to
keep him warm out in the hills on cold, wet nights.
He had a white blaze and a white bib, and half-
cocked ears that were always vigilant for warning
sounds. He carried his feathered tail low, in the
habitual low profile that let him swivel quickly or
bunch his muscles for a quick burst of speed. Jack
was so smart, Bud boasted, he could drive those
sheep through the eye of a needle. And he never

5

harmed a one of the plaguey beasts, nor ever let anyone or anything else hurt one either. Jack was so smart, Bud swore down at the local, he could sense danger when it was two valleys away.

The only thing Jack never did understand was market day. He and the boys and the other dogs brought the sheep to whatever place Bud told them and then . . . nothing. No sheep, no job, just a saucer of ale on the floor of the tavern.

Now, Squire Randolph wasn't too stuck up on his own worth to bypass the local alehouse on his way home through Sheltonford village, nor to share a mug with his tenant, nor to admire Bud Kemp's fine working dog. The two men had a lot in common, but this was not France. Neither man, in fact, would think of getting their dogs together any more than they'd encourage the sheepherder's sons to go courting the landowner's daughters. There was just no way in King George's England for Squire's Belle and Kemp's Jack to know each other, in the biblical sense, that is . . . except for Miss Sonia.

"But, Papa, they were only playing!"

Squire's bellow of rage could be heard two counties away. "Hell and damnation, Sunny, didn't I tell you I wanted Belle in the house tonight? I should have listened to your grandmother and beaten you years ago. It's not too late. I'll ship you off to boarding school, see if I don't!"

"But, but, Papa," she said, sniffing, "you just said Belle was to keep me company tonight because you had to go visit Mrs., um, someone on business." At his narrow-eyed look, Sonia hurried on, her bottom lip trembling. "And, and Belle missed her friends in the kennel so much, she was crying by the door."

"You are never, ever permitted to open the front door by yourself at night!"

Sonia shrank back from his roar, her blue eyes awash in tears. "I didn't, Papa, truly. Jack came around by the library door, you know, the one Taylor leaves open for you when you're coming home late from—from wherever you go. Isn't Jack clever, Papa?"

Squire Randolph sank down in an old leather chair in what used to be his orderly library, in what used to be his well-ordered life. He shook his head in resignation and motioned to Sonia, who promptly launched herself into his lap. "Ooph, poppet, you're getting too big for your poor old da. And you are surely too old to be in such scrapes. Why, you are all of ten now—"

"Nearly eleven."

"And country-bred. You know what happens when a, uh, ram and a ewe get together."

"Yes, Papa, but you didn't tell me that Belle was feeling motherly like you say about the ewes and the mares and the sows and the hens and—"

"All right, Sunny, I should have—"

"And I didn't know Jack was feeling frisky like you say when the stallion—"

"Enough! Here, blow your nose."

She took the handkerchief he held out to her, snuffled into it a few times, then squirmed around to look up at him, blue eyes shining despite the tear streaks, dimpled grin showing a missing tooth. "Papa, can I keep one?"

Squire Randolph was still saying "No" some two months later. "You know you cannot have one, poppet. They just wouldn't make good house dogs. They'd be too big, too wild. I'll buy you a puppy, love, see if I don't. What would you think of a little pug you can carry around? You know, with those cute little squashed-in faces? Or a Pekingese you can comb and brush and put ribbons in its hair. You'd like that, wouldn't you, Sunny?"

Sunny stamped her foot. She wouldn't like a lap dog at all. She was too old for dolls.

"No matter, the pups'll likely be sickly anyway."

And she was too old not to know what happened

to unwanted puppies and kittens. Someone would tell her the babies were sickly, and the next day they'd disappear. Not this time, she vowed.

The men in the stables were like jackstraws under the weight of Miss Sonia's desperate coaxings: they crumpled immediately. So she managed to be on the scene for the grand event and could see for herself that all three of the pups were strong and shiny, suckling avidly. Her eyes big with wonder, Sonia turned to share this marvel of new life with her father, and intercepted his signal to the head kennelman, Tom. Squire jerked his head once to the side, and Tom nodded.

Sonia ran to her father and clutched his hand. "No, Papa! No!" she cried in a pathetic little voice.

Randolph stroked her gold braids, tumbled, as usual, out of their ribbons. "I'm sorry, Sunny, but the bast—babies are neither fish nor fowl. You know they're no good for anything."

"No, I don't know that, Papa, and you don't either! You can't yet. Why, that would be like deciding someone was guilty before you heard the evidence. And you wouldn't do that, Papa, I know. Everyone says you are the fairest man in the shire. They made you magistrate, didn't they? You didn't even send Eddie Spears away when everyone knew he was poaching. No evidence. That's what you said, Papa. So you have to give Belle's puppies a chance, too."

The pups were weaned young, though not for lack of attention, despite Squire's best efforts. He wanted to avoid future disappointments and heart-wrenching scenes. But no governess or nanny or nursemaid had yet kept Miss Sonia from where she wanted to be, so she knew Tom's report before he gave it to her father.

"Very well, Sunny, we'll keep the blondish pup for now. Tom says she follows a scent right smartly for such a young bitch, and sticks to it. She won't

8

look so out of place with the pack, either. But she's not a pet, mind, and if she doesn't work out, she's gone. Now, let that be the end of it and these other two wretched whelps. I don't want to see them around here anymore."

Sonia patted his knee. "Of course not, Papa. Mr. Kemp will make sheepdogs out of them."

"I'll keep the spotted bitch, sir, Miss Sonia. Seems to take to the sheep. Quiet-like an' gentle with 'em." Kemp not-so-gently nudged the last pup, the only male, away from chewing on his heavy boot. "Not like this fool. Barked in their faces, he did, then ran the silly beasts in circles till we could catch 'em, and him no bigger'n a minute. I got no time for a dog what only wants to play."

The mostly black dog had noticed Squire's riding crop, tap-tapping against Randolph's thigh, and was lunging at it, trailing mud and straw and other stable debris down the well-clad leg. Squire kicked him away. Ferocious infant growls turned to a soft whimper as the squire nodded sagely. "My man Tom had no better luck with him. He wouldn't stay on a scent, just hared off in twenty directions at once. Wouldn't bring a stick back, so he'd never make a retriever, and he sure as Hades isn't quiet enough to go on point." Squire turned to his daughter to make his final, sad ruling in the case.

And there she was, his baby, his heart's ease, sitting cross-legged on the stable floor amid the muck, with a miserable mutt on its back in her muddied lap, teething on one of her blasted braids!

"I'm sorry, poppet, but there you are. No one wants this one."

She looked up at him, his angel, with that smile so like her mother's, and his eyes almost watered. Then she declared, in a tone of voice also reminiscent of Allison Harkness Randolph: "I do." She set the dog on his white feet and ruffled his shaggy black coat, pulled straw out of the arched and plumed tail with its white tip. She bent over and kissed the puppy right between his clownish gold eyebrows.

"But, Sunny," her poor father tried one last time, the same as he'd tried to convince Allison her sons did *not* need to be sent to boarding school, or that fox hunting *was* pious enough for a Sunday. "But, Sunny, he's not good for anything!"

"He's good enough for me."

And that is how I, Fitz the dog, by Jack out of Belle, came to share my life with Miss Sonia Randolph.

Chapter Two

They named me Fitz, which in ancient times was used to denote a blot on the family escutcheon, the old bar sinister, a product of an unsanctioned joining. A bastard. Human persons seemed to care a lot about cat dirt like that. I didn't. After all, wasn't everyone always praising both my parents? What more could a body ask? My sire was the finest sheepdog between here and Canis Major. He could think like a sheep, they said. Then again, a *rock* could think like a sheep. Jack could think *for* a sheep, for a whole flock of sheep and for the shepherds, too. And my dam never lost a fox. A few horses, their riders, the master of the hunt, but never the fox. No, I had nothing to be ashamed of in my forebears. In fact, I wanted to be just like them.

But sheep? Moving them from place to place to place, when all they talked about was grass and grass and grass, just to let the harebrained shepherd lose them for you? That made no sense to me, no more than fox hunting did. You kill the foxes and what do you get? More rats. And everyone knows what you get then, and it's not just the bubonic plague.

Still, I yearned to fulfill the promise of my breeding, to go beyond mere existence toward excellence. I looked around and there she was, Miss Sonia Randolph. I knew right away—they say it's like that with true vocations—that I had found my calling. I was going to be a companion! Not just any companion; I was going to be the best companion since Hector was a pup.

Please note that I consider myself a companion, not a pet to be pampered and sheltered, smothered and caged for another's pleasure. I accept my soft bed, my regular meals, but I work for them, training Miss Sonia.

There were no more tantrums. Miss Sonia soon learned that *I* would be banished to the stables for her misbehavior. There were no more missed sessions in the schoolroom either, and no more unfinished lessons. If Miss Merkle was pleased in the mornings, Miss Sonia quickly deduced, then Papa was pleased at luncheon, and we were free to do as we pleased for the afternoon.

No one ever needed to worry about us when we were out and about. Where I was, she was. Where she was, I was. No one had to feel guilty that there were no other children for Miss Sonia to play with, or had to take a groom away from his chores just to shadow her about. No one had to worry about the eggs disappearing from the henhouse or the vegetable garden being torn up, either. I was a responsible dog now; people trusted me. They knew that, like my mother, I would never get us lost and, like my father, I would defend Miss Sonia to the death.

We went everywhere. We knew every bird nest, every new foal, every gingerbread baker and sausage maker for as far as we could go and still get home in time for supper. We *never* missed supper.

It was a time to learn, a time to talk. We had discussions with birds, beasts, bugs, even bats. Socrates' cave had nothing on theirs!

As time went on, we were more on our own. Miss Catherine completed her schooling and her Season with honors: a ring from Lord Martin Backhurst, marquess, from Bath. Master George left university to study the bachelor life in London; Master Hugh became Lieutenant Hugh Randolph, posted to Portsmouth. And we expanded our horizons. The pianoforte, watercolors, the reins of a pony cart, the reins of the household, it was all the same. We knew which groom to chivy, what new tweeny needed a kitten in her bed so she wouldn't be homesick, where the sun cast the prettiest shadows, and when Papa liked to hear "Cherry Ripe." We kept growing, learning. I even stopped teasing Deer Park's tame deer. They were too easy.

Squire Randolph was happy. He threw into the trash Lady Atterbury's letters demanding that he send Sonia away to school before the provincial hoyden was permanently freckled. The neighbors were happy that there was a real lady at Deer Park, and Miss Sonia was happy. Why not? Everyone loved her.

I loved her, but I was not happy. I was five years old.

Five is not old for a dog; sixteen is not old for a human person like Miss Sonia. But I worried. We were no longer ignorant children. I, at least, had learned from everyone around me— sparrows and sows, milkmaids and meadow mice—that there is a higher purpose beyond mere survival, beyond even personal success. We each have another calling, a universal—

dare I say divine?—raison d'être. Succession. We must carry on.

Sirius knows I was doing my share, and so were those maids out behind the barn, but Miss Sonia was sixteen, and playing chess with her father.

But enough of teleology. I once knew a badger who fancied himself a philosopher. Fellow could bore the fleas off a ferret. I decided to take matters into my own paws. As soon as the family returned from London, I was going to start holding up carriages.

The heir was getting married. George Randolph was taking in holy matrimony the hand of Miss Jennifer Corwith, and he was doing it with all pomp and glory at St. George's, Hanover Square, in full view of half the ton. According to Squire Randolph, smug in the first pew, the boy hadn't done half-bad for himself. Miss Corwith was a handsome enough female with a more-than-handsome dowry. She came from a good family—her mother's people were distantly related to royalty, but not so uppity that they could look down on George's ancestors. Squire scowled at Lady Almeria Atterbury seated next to him, looking more like a jewelry shop mannequin than a dowager duchess. Uppity didn't half describe his mother-in-law. He turned back to the ceremony. The bishop was still spouting incomprehensible eloquence.

The Corwiths were doing themselves up proud. Of course, this affair wasn't nearly as grand as the bash Squire threw for his Catherine's wedding. Then again, Catherine married the Marquess of Backhurst. The Sheltonford chapel in Berkshire had been laughingly dismissed, and a simple ceremony at Atterbury House was out of the question. Balls, breakfasts, bride clothes, Lady Almeria spared no expense. Why should she, when Elvin Randolph was paying? Roses were not good enough;

14

she wanted orchids. A handful of attendants was paltry; every classmate of Catherine's at Miss Meadow's Select Academy became a bridesmaid, it seemed, with every gown, slipper, and hairpiece added to Squire's account. And the reception after, well, the food could have fed every dirt-poor tenant in Berkshire for a year, if the wealthy members of society hadn't devoured it all in a matter of hours. He frowned again, this time encompassing the whole congregation of overfed, overdressed jackaninnies. Then his brow cleared.

It had all been worth it, to show the ton that Backhurst wasn't marrying down, by Jupiter, and to show Lady Almeria Atterbury that Elvin Randolph was no countrified coin clutcher. Mostly, though, it had been worth all the blunt, and the time and botheration, just to see his girls walk down that long aisle.

He didn't actually see Sonia, naturally, for as flower girl, she went before him and Catherine. And his Sunny didn't quite manage to walk down that white-carpeted path; she skipped. Flowers twisted into her hair, a gap-toothed grin for the bishop, the minx turned and winked at her brothers. Lady Atterbury clutched her vinaigrette the whole time.

Then came Squire's turn, with Catherine. He would never forget the joy on her face nor the hushed awe in the vast cathedral as he led to the altar the most beautiful bride in decades. Not since her mother, they whispered, and tears came to his eyes even now, at quite a different wedding, just remembering. He took out his handkerchief and blew his nose.

The dowager poked a bony finger in his ribs. "It's they who ought to be crying, you twit," she hissed, nodding across the aisle to the bride's family, "not you."

His collar was starched too high for him to look. He nodded, barely.

"My goddaughter heard that silly Corwith chit

didn't want anyone to compare her wedding with Catherine's—gel can't hold a candle to our Lady Backhurst—so she just picked two attendants. No chance of being cast in the shadow on her day in the sun that way, especially with Catherine stuck in Bath in her condition."

"You know what Backhurst said," the squire whispered back. "Maybe this time, if she stays quiet . . ."

Lady Atterbury twitched her scrawny body a hairbreadth away on the cushioned seat. "My granddaughter, sir, is not a barnyard creature whose breeding is subject to one of your interminable speculations."

Squire mopped his forehead with the linen he still clenched. "Sorry," he muttered.

The dowager nodded and edged closer so she could continue her conversation. There was nothing Lady Atterbury liked better than a good gossip, unless it was baiting her son-in-law, especially in church, where he couldn't raise his voice or flee to the stables.

"Vain as a peahen, that Corwith girl," the old lady confided. "So she chose her spinster stepsister from Corwith's first marriage as maid of honor. Leah's a plain, shy old ape-leader who never took. And for bridesmaid, Jennifer picked George's harum-scarum little shire-bred sister. Heh heh."

Squire shifted his eyes to see if anyone had heard the old harridan's cackling, then he checked to make sure Sunny hadn't brought a mouse into the church or had her petticoat dragging. No, she was standing there next to Hugh as pretty as when they'd left Atterbury House, for a miracle. Her golden curls were as bright as the braid on her brother's dress uniform. Those same curls, or most of them, anyway, were held up for the first time with a wreath of blue silk flowers. She wore her grandmother's pearls, her mother's smile, her sister's elegant charm—finally, thank heaven!—and that glow that was only Sunny's.

Minds might be wandering as the bishop droned on, but from what the squire could see, most eyes were on the altar where the bridal couple knelt, their attendants to either side. Unfortunately, no one was looking at the bride.

Lady Atterbury did not want Sonia at the wedding breakfast. "Chick ain't full-fledged yet," she said, excusing her granddaughter's early withdrawal. "We'll fire her off next year." Actually, the dowager wanted Sonia out of the way before the untutored chit did something outrageous to give the Quality a disgust of her, before the wedding toasts got too ribald, or before the bride murdered her. She made sure Sonia was escorted home as soon as politely possible.

The squire was not so lucky.

"That one is going to make a stir," the dowager announced to him after she'd dragged Randolph away from a gathering of cronies and a discussion of the latest improvements in crop rotations and opera dancers. "What are you going to do about it, Elvin?"

First he was going to rub his knuckles where she kept tapping them with her fan, then he was going to make sure he wasn't back in short pants. "Do about, uh, what, Lady Almeria?"

"About finding her a husband, you looby! That one could land a duke, if there was a decent one among the bunch, but she's as sure as salvation going to attract trouble like a magnet. And what are you going to do about it, Elvin? Are you going to find an eligible parti and arrange a good marriage before she lands in the basket? Or are you going to do what you've always done, and give the chit her head?"

"It's a good, level head, ma'am, not stuffed with gewgaws and gossip. Sunny's not more hair than wit like most females her age. She's a wise little puss."

"That's not enough, Elvin. You wouldn't send her to me, you wouldn't hire the females I recommended to school her properly, you wouldn't even send her to Miss Meadow's Select Academy that turned Catherine out so nicely. Sonia don't know how to go on. She could embarrass us all." Before her victim could work himself up to produce the ladylike governess Miss Merkle as a good loud parry, or deliver a thrust about London manners and mores, right there at his son's wedding reception, the dowager delivered the coup de grace. "Worse, planted like a cabbage out in Berkshire, she'll make a mésalliance."

She didn't say it. She didn't say, "like Allison." But he heard it, and his ruddy tan grew ruddier. "If Sunny wants to marry a farmer," he said through gritted teeth, "she has my blessing. She's got too much in her brainbox to fall for a here-and-thereian."

"She's got you wrapped around her finger, you mean, as always. The chit's got more energy and enthusiasm than a colt, and about that much sense of what she owes her name. What if she throws her bonnet over the windmill for some linendraper's assistant? What will you do then?"

He'd bellow the rafters down, that's what, the same as the Duke of Atterbury had done. And he'd swallow his own tongue before he admitted it to this diamond-decked she-devil. "Sunny's young yet; no need to worry about her marrying for ages."

"No? Well, you think about it, you twiddlepoop; you're not getting any younger!"

Squire Randolph did think about getting older, and Sonia getting older, and even that old-maid daughter in the Corwith household getting older. The only ones getting younger were the successive widows he kept in the cottage in the village. He thought about it on the carriage ride home, and looked around when they arrived in Sheltonford.

He looked at the local boys with new eyes and saw gangly gossoons and unlettered lumpkins. Then he compared his Berkshire friends' sons with his son's London friends he'd met at the wedding, and started sending out invitations. Surely among George's Corinthian set there'd be a young buck who could appeal to Sonia, appease Lady Atterbury, and not displease himself too much. Surely, when pigs flew.

"Never seen so many cow-handed fiddlers," he muttered into his newspaper at breakfast, after seeing off the latest of his invitees. This one limped so badly, he wouldn't even stay for the hunt, which was the ostensible reason for the blasted visit.

"What's that, Papa? Did Lord Northcote get off all right?"

"Just fine, poppet." Fine, except for a smashed curricle and worse-damaged ego. The poor fellow'd had to be carried up the drive, chicken feathers blowing out of his hair. Sunny's damn fool dog was barking to raise the dead, so Squire couldn't even get the viscount inside and cleaned up before she saw him. A viscount, deuce take it. He shook his newspaper. "What in the blazes were chickens doing on the roadway? That's what I'd like to know."

Sunny narrowed her eyes and looked sharply at the dog at her feet. She shook her head. No, it couldn't be. "Good dog, Fitz."

"That mutt's not begging at the table again, is he?"

"Of course not, Papa."

"Of course not, why should he beg? You feed him everything in sight anyway. And you cannot deny he caused Sir Findley to part company with his horse last week."

"Fitz was chasing a rabbit, Papa."

"Findley swore there was no rabbit, just a berserking wild beast."

Fitz had his head in Miss Sonia's lap, softly brushing his tail along the floor. She stroked back his shaggy eyebrows. "Of course he did. The silly

19

man couldn't very well admit he'd chosen to ride more horse than he could control. I think the problem is that while George's friends are sporting-mad, they are all city drivers. They're not used to our country roads. What was that other gentleman's name? The one who put his phaeton in the ditch just because a few sheep were blocking the road?"

"L'duc de Bourville," her father said with a groan.

Sonia came around the table to place a kiss on his cheek. "Are you very sorry you'll have no company on the hunt tomorrow?"

Sorry? He wouldn't be sorry if he never had to see any of the quick-tempered, bad-mouthed young bloods again, especially the one whose whining he had to listen to for a whole week before the sawbones declared him fit to travel. He wouldn't let a single one of the chubs call on his daughter. B'gad, he wouldn't let a man jack of them drive her the half mile to church! Perhaps he should tell Hugh to bring some of his officer friends home for his next leave. No, he couldn't bear the idea of his little girl off somewhere following the drum. Or of telling Lady Atterbury.

"Sonia." Squire only called her Sonia when he was troubled. She sat on the arm of his chair to listen carefully. "Sonia, your grandmother thinks it's time we started thinking about a Season for you. Perhaps you should spend some time with her in London, quiet-like until your come-out, you know, but meeting some of her friends', er, daughters, so you'll have acquaintances of your own when the time comes."

"You mean meet all those exquisite coxcombs, don't you? I know what Grandmama wants, and that's a fancy title, no matter that the sprig of nobility has less upstairs than an oak tree in winter."

Squire Randolph laughed and pinched her cheek. "What do you know of dandies and such, huh, puss?"

"I know Backhurst. Why, he buys more clothes in a year than most men buy in a lifetime. He's always complaining about his health, and he can't even give Catherine a ba—"

"Sonia!"

"Well, I never did see why she married him."

"Then you don't want to go stay with Lady Atterbury?"

"Heavens, no, Papa. You won't make me go, will you?" Sonia giggled. "Grandmama terrifies me."

"Me, too, poppet," he confessed. "Me, too. No, I won't force you to go. What would I do here without my sunshine?"

She slid into his lap and threw her arms around him for a hug the way she always did. "And I won't leave till Grandmama finds me a man just like you!"

Right, when hell freezes over.

Chapter Three

$\mathcal{I}$s there such a thing as hell? What about heaven? Are there sausages there? For that matter, is there a God? Many gods? There used to be pantheons of them, Osiris and Thor, Baal and Vishnu. Gods are immortal, so where did they go?

I wait outside the doors of the Sheltonford chapel every Sunday listening to the psalms and the hymns and the sermons, but I still do not understand this one omniscient, omnipotent being theory. I mean, look around. We've got rabies and hunger and fleas. Shouldn't someone get rid of the cat dirt if they've got the shovel?

Human persons have a great deal of imagination. That's a fact. Think of all their inventions, all their books, a heaven with no dogs allowed. Think about that cockamamie idea they cherish: that some divinity created us . . . to serve them. What a quirky sense of humor this creator must have had, making an entire horse just so some scribbler could glue his book together, teaching suchamany worms how to spin just so ladies didn't have to wear fig leaves. Hogwash! And what possible use could they have for gnats? Only mankind could subscribe to such a notion.

Yes, they are helpless, so we help them when we can, but that's as far as it goes. We kick dirt on this theory of dominion. Animalkind embraces the mysteries and worships only one religion: survival. My survival, my children's survival, my children's children's ...

So I ate a cat.

The honeymoon was over, the nuptial visits to aunts in Scotland and cousins in Ireland were complete. In other words, the bride was in a family way. George was ecstatic; he could be home for grouse season. Jennifer was less thrilled. She'd looked forward to at least another Season in town, this time with the freedoms of a married lady. At last she'd flirt with rakes, gamble at polite hells, wear bright colors. Now she was condemned to making eyes at the footmen and playing whist with her father-in-law. As for clothes, she might as well start ordering tents!

She swept into Deer Park prepared to hate it, and she was disappointed again. The mellowed brick manor house was handsome and set among lovely grounds and well-kept gardens. The furnishings were tasteful and the staff was polite. Even her new sister-in-law was properly deferential, personally escorting her upstairs to Jennifer's spacious and freshly decorated rooms. Jennifer's only recourse was to pick on the dog.

"I'm sorry, Sonia, but I cannot abide dogs in the house."

"Oh, dear, I'm afraid you'll have to get used to them. Father often brings his hounds in, you know." From the look on Jennifer's face, she obviously had not known. Sonia smiled and went on:

"Please feel free to call me Sunny as George and Father do. And I'm to call you . . . ?"

"Jennifer. This will never do. No, Sonia, I have to insist this . . . creature stays in the kitchens. I'll speak to Father Randolph about the hounds. I'm sure he'll understand. Why, Muffy wouldn't be safe." She shuddered dramatically and clasped her white fur muff more closely to her chest.

Muffy was a white long-haired cat with gold eyes and pushed-in face. She was as fat as she was lazy, content to be hauled around on Jennifer's hand warmer like a dowager on a sedan chair. Jennifer thought the cat and muff, especially when she wore her ermine-trimmed pelisse, gave her a cachet. Her signature, she called it, like Poodle Byng.

"Like Poodle Byng?" Sonia choked, trying to stifle her giggles. Right now poor endangered Muffy was doing a fair imitation of a cushion atop a burgundy velvet-covered slipper chair.

"Oh, I forgot you couldn't be au courant with what's à la mode in Town," Jennifer sniped, recognizing the younger girl's levity, "in notables or fashions."

Sonia fidgeted with the ribbons of her new dimity round gown, which her grandmother had sent down from London and she'd saved for this special day. She didn't reply.

"Nonetheless, I shan't have my dear Muffy distressed by any rowdy dogs."

Muffy had finished her pillow act and was now portraying a Staffordshire porcelain fireplace dog, batting Fitz aside to get the warmest spot on the hearth.

"Fitz is the gentlest creature on earth," Sonia said, scratching behind the dog's ears in consolation. "He would never hurt anything."

"But he sheds! I don't want any awful black dog hairs on my light-colored muslins."

Sonia just looked over to the burgundy velvet chair where white hairs clung like threads on a cutting table. "That's why Fitz is not permitted on the furniture. Nor are the hounds, of course. And we'll just have to make sure Muffy is in another room when Father brings them in. Is there anything else we can do to make you more welcome?"

Jennifer gave up, for now. "How do you stand it in the country, Sonia? What is there to do with all this time?"

Sonia didn't know how to answer, since studying with Miss Merkle, running the house, looking after the tenants, helping at the Sunday school, and keeping Papa company seemed to leave no free time at all. She was hoping George's wife would take over some of the responsibilities, but didn't want to discuss housekeeping on Jennifer's first day. She tried to remember what Catherine liked to do. "We have a lovely pianoforte, and a good library, and the church is always needing new altar cloths." No response. "We go riding, of course, and walking, and visiting with the neighbors. They are so anxious to meet you, I'm sure the vicar's wife and the Minch sisters will be over for tea Sunday."

"The . . . vicar's wife and the Minch sisters?" Jennifer threw herself on the bed. Sonia sank down on the rug between the cat and the dog, stroking both. She missed Jennifer's look of disgust.

"Oh yes, they run the lending library. And the postal office." Jennifer moaned, and Sonia hurried on: "We have card parties and dinners, and informal dances sometimes when there is company for the hunt. And there are assemblies over in Seldenridge, the nearest town of any size"—Jennifer brightened—"once a month."

"Oh." Jennifer stared up at the swagged canopy over her bed. "At least you have linendrapers and dressmakers, don't you?"

Sonia busied herself retying Muffy's bow, barely whispering: "Just the Minch sisters."

Jennifer shrieked.

"But they get all the latest fashion journals from

25

London, or Papa could have them sent with his newspapers, and . . . and there are lots of shops in Seldenridge. You could ride there anytime you want. George said you were a bruising rider. That's what first attracted him to you, he told us at the wedding."

Jennifer sniffled. "The physician said I mustn't ride anymore!"

"Then you can take the pony cart. Or maybe George will buy you a curricle of your own. Father says I am too young."

"I don't know how to drive a cart," the bride wailed. "I never needed to know, in the city."

Jennifer was sobbing now, and Sonia was patting her hand, pouring tea, ringing the bellpull. Fitz pushed the door open and left. "Oh dear. Don't cry, Jennifer. Please. I know, I'll teach you to drive. Then you won't need to call out half the stable staff every time you want to buy a new ribbon or go visiting. It'll be our surprise for George. What do you think of that?"

Sonia was thinking that George was in for more than one surprise. She was also wondering where she was going to find time to teach her bubble-headed new sister-in-law how to handle the ribbons. Anyone who would name a cat Muffy . . .

Jennifer sat up and clapped her hands. "How absolutely perfect! You shall teach me how to drive, and I shall teach you how to dress like a lady!"

Oh dear.

The new Mrs. Randolph—Mrs. George below-stairs and in the village—grew about as content as she grew competent at the reins. Coco, the old mare who was used to finding her own way home from the village while Miss Sonia drove with her nose in a book, seemed to have forgotten which foot went where. She did manage to find every rut and bump on the road to the village, however. When Jennifer finally reached Sheltonford, she was usually too queasy to step down outside the tiny emporium.

"Too high in the instep," Miss Petronella Minch declared.

"We won't call again," her sister, Miss Marietta Minch, added.

"But Miss Sonia serves such a lovely tea."

At first Sonia tried to keep Jennifer busy with driving lessons, renovations to the nursery, introductions to the local society. She even agreed to be poked and prodded and pinned into a new wardrobe of sheer muslins and soft silks, just so Jennifer could have the pleasure of talking fashions and fabrics for endless hours. Sonia still preferred her kerseymeres and calicos for the long walks and comfortable times she managed to fit in. She thanked her lucky stars that Jennifer slept late in the mornings and rested after lunch, so Sonia could get her own chores done. George's wife refused to look at the menus or go over the household accounts with Sonia, saying: "Oh no, you're still the daughter of the house and still your father's hostess."

As Jennifer's shape got more unwieldy, though, her temper grew more uncertain. She took her pettishness out on George when he was available, so he made himself less available, checking out new breeds of sheep in Weymouth or Wales or the West Indies, for all Sonia knew! With George off on his trips, Sonia was left to bear the brunt of Jennifer's spite, until Squire Randolph had the downy notion of inviting Jennifer's stepsister to Berkshire.

"You remember, that quiet gel from the wedding, Leah."

"Papa, you are brilliant! She seemed so pleasant and mild-mannered. Perhaps she won't mind Jennifer's megrims."

"I don't think she was very happy in London; might be glad for the change."

"It might be that she wasn't happy with Jennifer, but I'll write this very morning. Oh, I hope she comes, don't you, Father?"

Miss Leah Corwith came, and with her soft-spoken ways, charmed everyone, even Jennifer for a while, for Leah was able to relate all the news from London. She kept up a large correspondence, so was au fait with the latest on-dits. Miss Corwith pleaded to assist Sonia with the household, for she was used to keeping busy, she said, and felt like a hanger-on otherwise. She was a skillful whist player and an enthusiastic if not expert rider. She even liked dogs. Sonia and the squire and George and the staff thought Leah was wonderful; Jennifer thought she was useful.

Now that Leah was here to take over the drudgery of a chatelaine, Jennifer didn't have to be so tolerant of Sonia. She saw no reason why the heir's wife shouldn't sit at the head of the table or take precedence going into dinners with company. The villagers should not call during Jennifer's established nap time, nor ask for Miss Randolph. The servants should take their orders from the future mistress of Deer Park Manor, not from some half-grown hoyden whose hair was always falling down and whose gloves were always soiled, when she remembered to wear them at all. Mrs. George gave up trying to make a lady out of that sad romp. She even stopped advising Sonia about her clothes, after all the gentlemen noticed and admired the forward chit—and made Jennifer feel more like a bloated cow than ever.

Jennifer knew better than to complain to George or Father Randolph about Sonia—she saw the way they fawned on the girl—but she did not hesitate to complain about that dog.

The dog was spoiled, the dog was ungoverned. He was no proper pet for a lady of fashion, and he was certainly not a proper chaperon. Sonia had no business running around the countryside like a veritable draggle-tail gypsy with nothing but a mongrel for escort. She and that flea-hound were going to land them all in the scandal-broth. Besides, the dog was always underfoot. Jennifer could trip and lose the child. Fitz had to go.

George went to his father, and the squire went to Sonia, after a quick helping of Dutch courage from the brandy decanter.

"Give me a pregnant bitch or a mare in foal, poppet, I know what to do. But women get queer as Dick's hatband. It's more'n a man knows what to do."

Sonia had her arms folded over her chest and her chin thrust out.

"It's only till after the baby comes, Sunny."

"If Fitz goes, Muffy goes." She turned on her heel and left.

Squire had another glass of brandy. This was going to be one very long pregnancy.

Miss Sonia tried, she really did. She stayed in her room, she stayed in the kitchen, she even stayed in the schoolroom. Fitz stayed with her, of course. She stayed out of the house till her nose turned blue and icicles hung off Fitz's fur; then she stayed in the warm stables, drying and brushing the dog till there wasn't a loose hair to fall out of that animal for a week. Jennifer took to putting her hands over her protuberant belly every time she saw Fitz, protecting the unborn babe.

Matters came to a head the day Jennifer refused to go to church in the family carriage if the dog came along, even if Fitz rode with the coachman as he'd done since her arrival.

"It is not seemly," she said, waving her fur muff around. "I refuse to be a laughingstock in the village where I expect to live the rest of my life." And she sat right down on the hall bench, put her muff on the floor beside her, and started untying her bonnet.

The servants disappeared. George was scarlet-faced with embarrassment, and Miss Corwith was suddenly memorizing her hymnal. The older Randolph looked beseechingly at his daughter. Sonia looked back at her father, and for the first time saw not a hero, not a god, just an ordinary, peace-loving, incompetent male. She looked outside; it was raining too hard to take the pony cart. She looked at the clock; they were already too late for her and Fitz to walk. She looked at Fitz; yes, he'd race them to town no matter what, meet them on the church steps, and likely shake raindrops all over Jennifer's ermine-edged pelisse. "Very well," she said, gesturing for them all to precede her out the door, and quickly. "Fitz stays home. This time." She never looked at Jennifer at all.

Squire invited the Pinkneys to take luncheon with the family after church. The Pinkneys were prosy old windbags, but a man couldn't be selective when he was looking for a smoke screen. Before they were all out of their carriages and inside the door, General Pinkney was bending George's ear with the same old tales of the Mahratta Wars. Mrs. Pinkney was giving Sonia and Miss Corwith her interpretation of the vicar's sermon. The host followed last, escorting his daughter-in-law at her slower pace. It wasn't until they were all gathered in the hall to hand over their wraps that Fitz came slinking down the stairs.

The big black dog didn't bound down the hall to welcome Sonia the way he usually did if she left him home. Furthermore, he wasn't quite as black and shiny as when they'd left. Instead he seemed to have played in the snow, only there was no snow on the ground. He didn't bark his usual welcome, either. He couldn't, his mouth was full. A piece of something white and furry dangled from between his long, white fangs. A piece of—

"Muffy!" Jennifer screamed. And screamed and screamed for two hours solid until the doctor could be found, out by Peg Wilson's. Not even dangling Muffy in her face, *felis intactus*, could halt the hysterics. George scrambled around finding bits and pieces of ermine skin and satin lining to prove the hand muff's demise. Miss Corwith burnt feathers. The squire suffered a very boring luncheon with the Pinkneys . . . and Miss Sonia wrote a letter to her sister in Bath, accepting Catherine's long-standing invitation.

A few days later Sonia burst headlong into her father's study the way she used to when there was a new litter of pigs, or the first dewdrop was out.

"Papa, is it true? Did you really tell George to hire some workmen to fix up the Dower House? Oh, Father, that's the best idea you've ever had! Now things can get back to normal."

"Whoa, poppet. Don't go crammin' your fences. Things are never going to be the way they used to be. We're all older now, Sonia. We have to think about the future."

"Yes, Papa." She knew to be quiet and listen when the squire was in such a serious mood. She took the seat across from him, her hands carefully folded in her lap.

"A man gets lonely when his wife is gone, his children are grown." He held up his hand when she started to speak. "No, hear me out. If not today, someday you'll want a husband, babies, a home of your own, and this isn't it. And that's the way it should be, like chicks leaving the nest. George and Jennifer will do better on their own, too. She'll settle down as soon as the baby comes, you'll see. Then I'll have no one."

"You'll always have those widows in the village."

The squire dropped the pen he'd been holding. "Tarnation, you shouldn't know anything about any— And you sure as hell shouldn't mention 'em! Didn't anybody teach you anything?" He looked away from the knowing smile she flashed him. "That's neither here nor there. What I wanted to say was, I'm thinking of stepping into parson's mousetrap myself. With Miss Corwith. Leah."

"That's just wonderful, Papa," she said, beaming. "I am so happy for you, truly. She's a lovely girl—uh, woman—and I think she will make you an excellent wife. And we already get along, so you'd never have to—"

"I know you like Leah, and she likes you. I wouldn't have her else, and she says she won't have me unless you give your blessings. You do, don't you, Sunny?"

Sonia giggled. "I thought the young man was supposed to ask the father's blessing. Of course I wish you every happiness!"

"Good, good. We're going to have a quiet wedding right here as soon as the banns are read. I mean, no reason to wait, at our ages. Might even start a new family. Leah's not much older than Catherine, after all. But the fact is, Sunny, you'd always be mistress here. And Leah's so gentle and kind, she wouldn't even mind. But it's not fair to her."

"I see, I think. I was planning on visiting Catherine anyway, so I'll just stay in Bath until Jennifer's baby is born and you and Leah are all settled in." She forced a laugh. "Perhaps I'll even nab some rich old duke there taking the waters, and make Grandmama happy."

Squire didn't join her laughter. "Thing is, Sunny, I wrote your sister a few weeks ago. Got a letter back today. She's finally increasing again and says she's too sick to take you around or anything, and can't jeopardize the baby, after so many disappointments. And, well, you never did get on with Backhurst. Catherine's just not up to that kind of brangling."

"I never did see why she married that milksop," Sonia muttered, studying the design on the Aubusson carpet—and her options. She swallowed, took a deep breath. "Grandmama?"

Her father nodded sadly. "Lady Atterbury."

Among wolves, only the dominant female gets to mate.

Chapter Four

$\mathscr{O}$f all the courtship rituals I have studied, the London Season sounds the most bizarre. My information comes from Muffy, the greatest feline impersonator of my experience. I have seen that cat portray a snowdrift, a dish towel, and a tea cozy. Such virtuosity!

According to Muffy, whose observations I cannot discount since she was witness to two Corwith sisters' come-outs before Jennifer's, human persons' mating behavior seems contrary to nature.

For one thing, the proper breeding age is arbitrarily set—by a committee, mind you—regardless of individual maturation. Then all of those selected (debutantes) to meet the most eligible males (catches) are herded together (the Marriage Mart) and dressed alike. In white, no less. The brightest colors, the most sparkly jewels, the finest plumage, are reserved for those who already have a mate! If a female loses her mate, she is forced to wear darkest black, even if she wishes to encourage another male.

In many species, the males fight for the females. Muffy says the London gentlemen often participate in fisticuffs, swordwork and marksmanship contests, even hold races. But the young women are not permitted to view these activities, or the unclad males, so how can they select the mate who is strongest, fittest, fastest, best able to protect them and their children? The debutantes are not permitted to be alone with the men, no, not even to dance more than twice in an evening with the same partner. How can they make a proper choice? No wonder they have so many ugly babies.

Muffy calls me naive. They choose for two things, she says, purity and property. The sexes are kept so firmly apart because chastity in females is valued above beauty or intelligence. There are chaperons and open doors and enough rules to choke a Chihuahua. This I can understand. A male wants to know that his own progeny will inherit his property, not some other stud's in the stable. The females accept this because property means possessions and power in London, and security for their families. A man does not have to be as brave as a bull, as strong as a stag, as fast as a falcon, as smart as a dog, to win the maiden of his choice. He has to be rich. The wealthier the female, the wealthier the male has to be to prove he can provide for her.

In her descriptions of the marriage contracts, Muffy has never mentioned anything about affection, devotion, or respect, which is not surprising for a cat. I question the absence of love in these negotiations, however, since mankind has made so much of that emotion over their centuries. Muffy just laughs. I shall wait until visiting Almack's to see for myself.

While I am looking forward to the Metropolis and exploring its possibilities, Miss Sonia does not share my enthusiasm. Her steps lag, her words come slower, her mouth droops. She grieves at the loss of her home, and I am sorry. I drop my bowl into her half-filled trunk to say, "Don't be afraid, I am coming with you." She smiles, but I can see she is sad. She's torn, having to leave her beloved father to make him happy, feeling guilt that his joy causes her pain. She does not understand: he is not her mate, she is not his dog. I lick her nose.

"Well, let me take a look at you, girl." The old lady raised her lorgnette and motioned for Sonia to turn around, like a horse on the auction block. "Now let me see a curtsy," she barked.

Sonia dipped into a bow suitable for royalty, and only ruined the graceful effect by making the obeisance to the dog at her side instead of toward her grandmother. Fitz lowered his head, as he'd been taught. Lady Atterbury made a sound almost like a chuckle. "You'll do. The hair is atrocious, of course, that sunburned skin is an abomination, and whoever had the dressing of you should take up upholstering. What do you think, Bigelow?"

Lady Atterbury's abigail, as venerable in her starched black uniform and lace apron as her employer was in taffeta and turban, made her own inspection. Sonia held her breath. "Monsieur Gautier. Lemon juice mixed with strawberries. Celeste's. Breathing lessons."

"See to it," the dowager said, as if making a silk purse out of a sow's ear overnight were as easy as matching ribbons. Lady Atterbury nodded to Bigelow, dismissing the poor woman to her Herculean task, then raised the looking glass again.

"And I suppose this is the animal that stirred the bumble-bath in the first place."

With a slight hand gesture Sonia had Fitz approach her grandmother's chair, sit, and offer his paw for shaking. Her Grace twitched her skirts aside. "A gentleman always waits for a lady to offer her hand first, Sonia. Remember that."

"Yes, Grandmama," Sonia said, ordering Fitz back to her side. "But he truly is a well-behaved dog. He won't cause anyone any trouble at all."

"Well, it's all the rage for ladies to carry their pets around with them. Margaret Todd even brought her parrot to tea at Devonshire House, I understand. All the unmarried women had to flee the room when it started to talk. I have a feeling you'll be an Original on your own, dog or no, but we'll see. Once the Season gets rolling, you'll send him back to Berkshire fast enough, I'm sure. He'll be company for you till the ball, anyway."

"The ball, Grandmama?"

"Of course; didn't think I'd fire you off without the proper *affaire*, did you? Invitation list is in the study; you can start on them tomorrow, after your fittings. Marston, he's the butler, don't you know, can help with the details, orchestra, refreshments, that type of thing."

"I . . . I'm to plan my own ball?"

"You don't expect me to do all that work at my age, do you? I'm too weak for that fardling nonsense. Don't get your garters in a welter; Marston knows how I like things. The ball will be in a month. Plenty of time. Bigelow should have you in shape by then. I've arranged with the war minister's wife to have your scapegrace brother here on leave to stand up with you. That clunch Elvin writes that he will still be on his wedding trip, and George cannot leave the milk-and-water miss he married. We cannot wait."

Sonia ignored the insult to her father; he'd warned her she'd better get used to them. "I'd be more than happy to delay the ball, Your Grace. Couldn't we just hold a quiet dinner, a small party?" she asked hopefully.

"Hmph. I know what's due the Harkness name, no matter if some don't. Wouldn't want those old gabble-grinders thinking I'm a lickpenny, would you?" She didn't wait for an answer. "Elvin's paying anyway. That's not to the point, girl. You are not Out till you've been presented to the queen and to the ton. And until you are Out, you can't *go* out. No balls, no picnics, no theater. I don't even want anybody seeing you looking like something that's been dragged through a bush backwards. Perhaps next week we might entertain some of my particular friends for tea."

"That sounds . . . lovely. May I at least go sight-seeing?"

"I am too old and frail to go gawking like a tourist at the Tower and Astley's Circus, and it ain't fitting for you to go with no one but servants. You'll make friends at your ball, gentlemen who will be in alt to escort you to such pawky places. In a group, of course. My goddaughter Rosellen has agreed to take you around with her after your presentation, so I won't have to drain my strength with those routs and venetian breakfasts. Lady Conare, Rosellen is now. She's good ton even if Conare's only a baronet. Carlton House set, don't you know, and only one away from the earldom now."

Sonia did not care about routs or the Regent's friends; she couldn't bear the idea of three weeks in the house with this crusty old tartar. Grandmama was about as frail as medieval armor. "Fitz will need exercise, Your Grace."

"You may take him to the park. The one in the square, of course, not Hyde Park, where you'd be ogled by every half-pay officer and libertine on the strut. Nothing will ruin a gel's chances faster. You'll take servants with you, naturally. We'll hire a groom and a maid for you. No reason to disturb my regular staff."

"But, Grandmama, I'll be safe with Fitz, and I am used to doing for myself."

Lady Atterbury rapped Sonia's knuckles with her lorgnette. "And I am used to being obeyed, young lady. You kick up a dust and I'll send you off to that academy in Bath so fast, you'll be there before Miss Meadow gets the note saying you're coming. You will go to the park and no further, you will wear a bonnet at all times so you lose that gypsy complexion, and you will always be accompanied by servants. Is that understood?"

Sonia bowed her head. "Yes, Your Grace." She thought of one appeal Lady Atterbury might heed. "But the expense . . ."

"Elvin can afford it. Better he spend his blunt on you than squander it on that young filly."

Sonia had already heard the dowager's opinions on her father's remarriage. All of Grosvenor Square must have heard. Before she was dismissed into Bigelow's charge, Sonia was treated to another lecture about what was due the family name, the Harkness name, that is. Grandmama felt the Randolphs could go to hell in a hand basket, and the sooner her granddaughter shed that label, the better. Here she shook her finger under Sonia's nose, saying: "And I won't have you throwing yourself away on any soldiers, scholars, or starving second sons."

Gamblers and gazetted fortune hunters were also forbidden, as were rakes, widowers, and Americans. Nabobs might be tolerated if they were Oxford-educated, and émigré French aristocrats, if their property had not been confiscated. Lady Atterbury did not bother to mention the rising London merchant class nor, in a rare moment of noblesse oblige, the gentry. Welcome, of course, were wealthy peers, preferably above the title of baronet. Impoverished noblemen were only slightly less acceptable, since the duchess was not unreasonable and there were more of the latter than the former. Sonia was well dowered enough, if the title was noble enough. After all, that's the way things were done in the *belle monde*.

"But don't think I mean to push you into a marriage you cannot like, Sonia. Those gothic forced marriages just create the foundation for scandal. No, I'll make you the same offer I made Catherine. If you cannot find a suitable gentleman to wed, you may stay on here as my companion."

"Well, now I know why Catherine married Backhurst." Sonia had conferred with Marston and confirmed appointments with Bigelow. She had taken tea with Lady Atterbury after the dowager's nap—no second servings, fidgeting, or feeding the dog. She had enjoyed a fifteen-minute airing in the park with Fitz—no running, shouting, or talking to strangers—and was finally sitting alone in her bedroom with something on her face that smelled like what the pigs got, if there was nothing better for them. She couldn't even hug her own dog, because he was too clever to get near her. She could talk to him, though, the way she always did.

"Do you know what I think, Fitz? I think I hate it here. All this effort and extravagance for a ball I didn't want in the first place. And for what?"

Fitz thumped his tail.

"To show off an expensive piece of goods to discerning buyers! That's all this is, you know. Grandmama means me to land a title to make up for Mama's 'lapse.' She thinks my portion is bait enough for a viscount at least, especially when dangled alongside the Harkness connection." She sighed. "She's most likely right."

Sonia scrubbed the mess off her face as though she could wash away the disquieting thoughts. When she was finished she sat on the floor with her arms around Fitz and watched the fire burn down in the grate.

"Well, I don't care. I'm not going to let her sell me off to the highest bidder, and I'm not going to stay here as her lackey either! I'll marry the first nice man I meet, see if I don't. I don't want any stiff-rumped nobleman looking down his nose at me and Papa, always expecting me to act the lady. And I don't care if he's poor. In fact, I might like him better if he needs my money, for then he might be more manageable about the settlements."

A few minutes went by while she thought, then: "He has to be pleasant, of course, and he absolutely must prefer the country. On the other hand, perhaps I could use my money to purchase a country estate—nothing too grand, naturally—and he could use the rest to stay in the City. That might be even better. We could work it out later." She yawned. "He should have a nice smile . . . and smell good."

So I dragged in the butcher's delivery boy.

Chapter Five

$\mathcal{W}$hat is beauty? What is the mystery of one creature's attraction to another?

Someone likened truth to beauty, but you cannot taste truth, or touch it, or feel it. It won't get your heart thumping, your pulses racing. It won't lick your ear. Besides, what a frog might find fascinating won't hold true for the titmouse. Then again, human persons find beauty in daubs of paint, chunks of marble, and Italian sopranos. Who can understand taste?

Take ticks, please. No one likes the bloodthirsty little buggers, no one finds them the least attractive—except other ticks. I truly believe this is where love enters the equations. The ugliest equine in horsedom could be grazing in the field, all swaybacked and moth-eaten, but let that mare come into season, and the stallion is in love. Old Gigi is the most beautiful creature he's ever seen. The sap rises, his heart sings. If he cannot be with her, he'll die. That's love. That's the fire that lets creatures as silly as sheep perpetuate their species, and the flame that helps a lady starling select one gentleman out of a flock of a hundred identical males. It's magic.

If marriage has nothing to do with love, as Muffy so firmly believes, there is no reason for cosmetics or corsets, padded shoulders or hairpieces. Solicitors could handle the transactions. We could be home in the country. Instead we spend boring hours planning for balls—dancing parties, not the fun chase-me kind—and improving Miss Sonia's appearance. We are *not* laying a trap, as Miss Sonia so inelegantly puts it; we are kindling a blaze.

Obviously Ned the butcher's boy did not generate any warmth. No magic. I myself thought he smelled delightful; it seems Miss Sonia prefers a gentleman to smell of Hungary water or snuff. I admit I have made mistakes before, but he seemed to fit her specifications so well. I guess I was barking up the wrong tree.

Lady Almeria revived after the Watch left. The already too-long-suffering Marston took charge, clearing the front steps of curious bystanders and the entryway of slack-jawed servants. Next the butler paid off the butcher and saw that the delivery boy was reimbursed for a new pair of breeches, plus a handsome tip for the trouble. The unfortunate animal was remanded to house arrest in Miss Randolph's room, and young miss, still giggling, set off for her appointment with the dressmaker. Properly escorted, of course. Then, his duties discharged with what dignity befitted a ducal residence, Marston withdrew to the butler's pantry, firmly locking himself in with a bottle of the late duke's vintage port, not to reappear until dinner.

This was not what he was used to, no, not even when Lady Allison, Master Thorndike, and Viscount Harkness, the heir, were young. Lady Atterbury and the late duke—and Marston—agreed that children were best raised in the country, by some-one else. That was how the new little duke was be-ing reared, in the country with his mother and an entire army of nursery staff to see that he did not burn down Atterbury Hall. He would seldom be in London to cut up Marston's peace until he reached his majority. Viscount Harkness did not live long enough to succeed to the title, predeceasing his fa-ther due to overindulging in brandy and underes-timating a jump. He never got to see the son everyone said was in his image, and Marston was almost hoping he himself wouldn't be around to see the lad either.

In all of Marston's days at Atterbury House, there had only been one ignoble episode, that concerning Miss Allison and her would-be betrothed. The event was of such monumentally vulgar proportions, it was still spoken of at the nearest pub. Now Miss Allison's daughter was here for just one day, and Marston could never show his face at the Red Stag again.

Oblivious to Marston's distress, Miss Sonia was shopping. For once, she was enjoying the experi-ence. Madame Celeste did not make her feel like a cabbagehead, instead encouraging her—and her father's remorse-driven generosity—to create a style of her own.

"I can see that Mademoiselle is not in the usual mode," Madame understated when her newest cus-tomer blew into the shop. Miss Randolph, with tou-sled tresses and laughing blue eyes, had instantly pleaded that, if she absolutely had to wear white for her come-out, Madame would please find a way to make it different from every other white debu-tante gown.

Sonia had never had so much choice before, and the new styles were looser and more comfortable. Sunny thought she'd feel more herself in them. Ma-dame unerringly brought what was suitable for her coloring and situation, and wooden-faced Bigelow was an unobtrusive guide. "The blue to match the eyes. No frills; we have nothing to hide. Colors are unexceptionable for daytime."

Sonia held up a fashion plate of a gown cut daringly low, winking at the assistant who was standing by to record the order. Madame Celeste clucked her tongue and threw her hands in the air, but Bigelow did not fail Sonia. "Haymarket ware." Sonia and the girl laughed, until Madame frowned at them.

After Sonia was measured, two ready-made gowns were presented for consideration. "An improvement," Bigelow decreed, so Miss Randolph was helped into the peach muslin in order to complete her shopping with less embarrassment to her grandmother's abigail. Best of all, Aimee, the shopgirl, was found to be of a size and shape with Miss Randolph, and was willing to stand in for all but the final fittings. Sonia handed the girl a handsome douceur. "Just please do not use it on so many strawberry tarts that I'll have to undergo those hours of pinpricks," she said, laughing.

"*Mais non*, mademoiselle, I save for my *dot*. Better a girl make a good marriage than make a good meal, *n'est-ce pas?*"

Further stops saw the crested coach fill up with bonnets and boots, fans and feathers, parasols and petticoats, stockings and . . . gloves. Sonia still had energy left to visit Gunther's to see about ices for the ball, and a florist to order the flowers. Bigelow was limp on the facing seat for the ride back to Atterbury House. "Youth" was all she said.

Monsieur Gautier called that afternoon. The coiffeur studied Miss Randolph from every angle. He lifted a curl, he let a wave drift through his fingers. He chewed his mustache. Then he began to cut. He cut and he cut, muttering all the while. Sunny was beginning to wonder how many sheep Bud Kemp could have shorn in this time when the slender Frenchman stood back, kissed his fingertips, and proclaimed, "A la cherubim." He had to pause to wipe his eyes. "I am a genius."

Sonia shook her head and felt three pounds lighter. She laughed in delight. Then she finally turned to look in the mirror. "Oh, sir, you are." What had been unruly wisps and wayward locks was now a golden halo of naturally and Gautier-tumbled curls, curls that couldn't fall down or fly away. They framed her face, revealing the high cheekbones and ready dimples. Her blue eyes sparkled even brighter. Not quite an angel, not quite an imp, and very, very appealing.

"What do you think, Fitz?" Hearing his name, the dog ran over and barked, bestowing the cut hair more liberally around himself and the room. "And, Bigelow, do you like it? Do you think Grandmama will? What about the gentlemen?"

"Yes. Yes. Heaven help them."

The next major project, in addition to writing out two hundred invitations, hiring an orchestra, and planning a menu, was finding servants. One of the underfootmen was promoted—or not, depending on who you asked, Marston or Bigelow—to be Miss Sonia's personal man. Redheaded Ian was big, strong, and liked dogs.

An abigail had to be hired from an agency. Bigelow thought they should request an experienced older woman to pilot Miss through the shoals of society. Marston wanted to hire a warden from Newgate. Sonia selected her own maid partly because Maisie Holbrook had freckles and partly because she looked as if she needed the job. Holbrook's last mistress had suddenly eloped—"with no connivance from me, on my honor, ma'am"—and Miss Martingale's parents had turned the abigail off without a reference. The position was secured when the neatly dressed young woman, not very much older than

46

Sonia, said, "That's a fine-looking dog, ma'am. Can I walk him for you sometimes?"

At first Maisie and Ian were inclined to be over-protective, especially after receiving their instructions from the dowager duchess, through Marston and Bigelow. Ian was terrified of all three of them, and Maisie knew another social misstep would end her own career. Ian insisted on holding Fitz's lead in the park, lest Miss Randolph be tugged or tripped. Maisie wanted to fuss for hours over Miss Randolph's hair and clothes.

Sonia swayed the pair to her way of doing things with two simple sentences: "Lady Atterbury does not pay your wages. I do." After all, she was Allison Harkness's daughter. So she got to Astley's Amphitheater and the Menagerie and London Bridge and the cathedrals with no one the wiser, and struck up friendships with flower girls and pie-men and the Watch and a kindly old gentleman who fed the squirrels in the park. He didn't even mind that Fitz chased the squirrels away, as long as he didn't catch any.

Lady Atterbury was pleased with her grand-daughter's progress. Bigelow judged her passable, and Marston was relieved there were no further Incidents. With more than a fortnight still to go before the ball, they deemed her ready to get her feet wet with minor socializing, to test the waters, so to speak, at small, private gatherings of the dowager's set. Sonia nearly drowned from boredom.

Lady Atterbury's crowd was not comprised of the great hostesses of the day, the Almack's patronesses and such. Her coterie contained instead those powerful figures' mothers and aunts and *belles mères*. The old beldams were therefore an even greater force to be reckoned with. They got together of an afternoon for silver loo, charitable committee meetings, musicales, poetry readings, and scientific dissertations. They also served up the latest gossip along with their tea and culture.

Sonia was not expected to participate in the conversations, thank goodness. In fact, she was often waved away to a secluded corner after her appearance and demeanor were scrutinized, lest her innocent ears be sullied. Many of the ladies refused to carry their ear trumpets, however, so the conversations were perforce loud enough not only to reach Sonia, but to rise above Herr Mitteldorf's performance on the harpsichord. Few of the grandes dames could rise without a footman's help after the performance, in fact, and fewer could see Herr Mitteldorf at all without their spectacles or looking glasses. Sonia thought she must be the only one there with all of her teeth, until she noticed another young woman across the way, concentrating not on the music or the chitchat, but on the book in her lap.

The young woman read her way through a lecture on the electrical properties of wool carpets, and through a dramatic presentation of an endlessly epic poem by a lisping young man with flowing locks.

Sonia made sure she sat near the young lady at the next gathering, a report from the directors of St. Bartleby's Institute for the Destitute, to which no one listened. The girl, for she could not be much older than Sonia, did not raise her eyes from her book, but she did reach into her reticule and pull out a matching purple-covered volume. "Here," she said, "you'll need this."

"This" was a purple-prosed gothic from the Minerva Press, and the young woman was Blanche Carstairs.

"Lady Blanche if you care for those things," Sonia's new friend and literary advisor introduced herself at the intermission. "I'm a countess in my own right, but don't let that bother you. I don't. It's one of those ancient land-grant titles that can pass through the female line. That's my aunt over there, the one in puce who is snoring."

Blanche—they were quickly on a first-name basis—was a drab, graceless type of girl, with little conversation and less fashion sense, but she knew everything. She flipped the pages of her book. "They think I'm not listening, so they say anything. Like how you're expected to make a grand alliance, despite coming from the gentry, if you don't make a mull of things."

Sonia gasped in indignation, but Blanche held her hand up. "It don't fadge. They"—she nodded toward the clusters of crones—"say I won't take, especially being fired off the same time as you, but Auntie says the lands and title will turn the trick. Of course, my dowry isn't as large as yours."

"Do you mean they all know the size of my dowry?"

"Goosecap, they all know the size of your shoes!" Blanche went back to her book. Sunny shrugged, then opened hers.

Some new, younger faces were added the afternoon Grandmama held open house. The old ladies trotted forth spotty-faced, stammering grandsons just down from university, bored middle-aged bachelor sons, and the occasional rakish man-about-town nephew who owed his living to the ancient relative.

"The hounds are on the scent," Blanche commented, making Sonia smile. They'd reluctantly put their books away for the afternoon. Sonia liked reading about the dashing heroes and put-upon heroines far more than she did pouring tea and listening to empty chitchat and insincere flattery.

Sonia finally got to meet Grandmama's goddaughter Rosellen Conover, Lady Conare, a brittle young matron who covered her slightly faded beauty in flamboyant dress. Rosellen was supposed to chaperone Sonia for the season. The older woman's eyes narrowed to slits when she saw Miss Randolph's fresh young beauty.

"Why, Lady Almeria, whatever can you be thinking?" Lady Conare chided. "Surely the chit's too young to be presented. She looks a veritable schoolgirl. Or a little milkmaid."

Lady Atterbury just cackled and waggled her sticklike finger under the woman's nose. "Told you she was a Diamond, didn't I?"

Lady Atterbury's assessment was quickly and eloquently seconded by Lady Rosellen's escort and brother, Lord Ansel, Baron Berke. The baron was a fairly attractive man of about thirty, trim if not muscular, and exquisitely tailored. There was just a touch of dandyism in his patterned waistcoat, crossed fobs, and heavy scent. Nor could Sonia appreciate the way he looked at her through his quizzing glass. Still, he was friendly and polite, and his compliments went far to restoring Sonia's confidence after his sister's cutting remarks. She was further impressed with Baron Berke when she saw him cross to where Blanche sat alone and unpopular—until she spoke to her friend later as they exchanged books.

"Berke? He's one of the season's catches, you know. They say his pockets are to let, so he's bound to settle on some heiress or other this year."

"Are you sure? He certainly didn't look like he was all to pieces."

"Don't be a goose. The worst wastrel in town can dress elegantly; he just don't pay his tailor. Berke's not that bad off. Yet."

"Well, he seemed pleasant enough."

"Of course he did; he'd never land an heiress else, title or no! Did he tell you that you were a breath of springtime, a bud of perfection just waiting to open? Did he kiss your hand and say he was honored to be among the first to touch the bloom?"

Sonia giggled. "You, too? Oh dear, and I thought he was the nicest of the gentlemen here today."

"You mean he was the only one with any conversation at all, even if it was Spanish coin. They"—Blanche nodded toward where her aunt and Lady Atterbury had their heads together—"say he was dangling after a rich Cit's daughter, but he'd sooner take you with your looks and money, or me for the title and lands. Do you think you'd have him?"

Sonia laughed, saying, "After you convinced me not to believe a word he says?" She tapped the book in her hand. "I'd rather have Count Rudolpho than a husband I couldn't trust!"

So, like Diogenes, I set out to find an honest man.

Chapter Six

I was taught that honesty means I am not to sleep on the furniture, even if no one is home. Honesty means not taking food from the kitchen when Cook isn't looking, unless it falls on the floor. I am a good dog.

Human persons are different. They make laws about honesty and then they break them. Sometimes this is a crime, sometimes not. Poaching happens to be a crime, but it is also dishonest—and confuses the game animals. Squire Randolph was very strict with poachers, yet he had no scruples about telling lies: "Here now, Bossy, we're just going to borrow your pretty little calf." To excuse these moral lapses, humans call them social lies, white lies, flummery. For Spot's sake, even poor color-blind Bossy can recognize a faradiddle when she hears one.

They do it all the time, calling such falsehoods polite fibs: "Delighted to see you. So glad you could call. You are looking lovely. I adored your gift. Please come back soon." Miss Merkle explained that gentlemen and ladies bend the truth a shade here and there so no one's feelings will be hurt. When the knacker comes and they tell the decrepit old plow horse, "Here, boy, we're just going to take a little walk," you know something more than feelings are going to be hurt!

No wonder animals have learned to distrust men. Still, I say don't listen to the words, listen to the heart. An animal can tell the truth. Just like I listened to what Lord Ansel Berke didn't say.

I was waiting in the hall when company came, quiet so Marston would not notice. Having studied under Muffy, I was pretending to be a scatter rug. Not my finest role, but I was not dragged back to the kitchens. Miss Sonia spotted me right away—she always does—when she walked some of the departing guests to the door. As soon as Marston turned his back to fetch Baron Berke's gloves, hat, and walking stick, she introduced us. We shook hands. He patted my head and said, "What a fine dog, Miss Randolph. Smart and handsome." Then he wiped his hands on a cloth.

He did not commit a crime, like stealing eggs from a chicken coop, or a sin, like stealing the chickens. But he does not have a true heart. A dog always knows.

Miss Sonia deserved better, so I had to expand our horizons. Somewhere in this great city of London . . .

I had never been on foot beyond the park before. Always we went sightseeing in the carriage, and I waited on the box with the driver outside the Tower or Westminster, marveling at mankind's achievements and wondering why they bothered. I could only sniff at the passing strangers from my high perch; now I would be down among them. I was looking forward to exploring on my own while Miss Sonia had her final fittings. Tippy the turnspit dog says there are rats as big as cats!

I saw one myself, a surly fellow with a half-chewed ear. He wouldn't give me the time of day, much less any hints as to where I should begin my search. Muffy was right, city folk aren't as friendly, for even the horses didn't stop when I asked directions. The heavy workers were short-tempered beasts in a great rush to get nowhere that I could tell. The fancier cattle were all twitchy nerves and bunched muscle, ready to explode. I stopped asking. I kept going, following my nose as it were, and oh, the smells! And the sights and the noise and the traffic. Even the air had myriad tastes. And men, hustling, bustling, busy. A few glanced my way, one tried to kick me, another held out a cup—and it was empty! Mostly they were in a hurry. I may have been a tad optimistic about my search.

I always knew where I was, of course. Hadn't I been carefully marking my way? Much too soon, though, I had spent every penny, out of sheer excitement, I suppose, so I decided to return home. But there were buildings in the way and high fences, and alleys no dog should walk down by himself. The smoke was so thick, I could not even sniff my own scent in the air, and a pair of livery horses pulling a hackney poked fun when I asked my way back to Grosvenor Square.

" 'Ere now, who's 'e think 'e is, some poodle wot gets 'is blinkin' toenails painted?"

"Oi say 'e ain't no gennlemun's dog, 'e's one of those baa-baa baby-sitters. Ya wants th' sheep pens out Marlybone way, ya 'airy botfly."

I wished them high hills and heavy loads, then I showed them my heels.
Did Diogenes ever get lost?

"Damn and blast! First those fools at the surgeon general's and now this!" The curricle was stuck in traffic, between a mail coach with a bunch of unruly schoolboys on top and a barouche whose high-pitched occupant was obviously no better pleased than the officer at the curricle's ribbons. Most likely some high-priced cyprian en route to her lover, he deduced from the garish red and gold trim on the outside of the expensive turnout, and the unladylike expressions coming from within. The officer cursed again, that he'd have time to listen to the high flyer's entire repertoire before this mess was cleared.

Gads, how he hated the city! He hated everything about it, including those clunches at the War Office who wouldn't send him back to Portugal without the medicos' approval. They, and that popinjay from the Cabinet, wanted him to sell out now that he'd come into the title. As if England needed another blasted nobleman more than the general needed him at the front. As if he ever asked to be earl in the first place. He cursed his brother Milo for up and dying. Well, he'd told them he wasn't selling out yet, and he wasn't using that damned title while he was in uniform. Major Darius Conover, Lord Warebourne whether he acknowledged it or not, was barely holding his high-bred cattle in check, and his temper not at all.

His batman, Sergeant Robb, got down to soothe the impatient bays, and to put a distance between him and the major's ill humor. The major liked to throw things when he was in a taking, and Lord knew, there wasn't much in a curricle to toss.

Church bells chimed the hour, and Major Conover whacked his driving whip onto the floorboards.

"Dash it, I told my nieces I'd drive them in the park this afternoon. Now they'll hate me even worse!"

Thinking he might do better to soothe his employer after all, Robb said, "Here now, Major, them tykes don't hate you, they hardly know you. They're just upset, both parents poppin' off like that, and then bein' shipped to relatives what didn't want 'em, and now landin' back here with you. It's no wonder the little ones are confused."

"Confused? That's gammon. The baby Bettina cries if I get near her, Genessa in the middle tries to kick me—my bad leg to boot—and the eldest, Benice, is so stiff and polite, I'm afraid she'll shatter into a million pieces one day." He beat his cane against the curricle's rail. "My blackguard of a cousin Preston and his bitch of a wife set them against me. Confused? I'm the one who should be confused. I've never been around children in my life!"

"You're doin' fine, Major. It just takes time."

"I don't have time, Robby. I want to go back and see Boney put down at last. And it's not as if I'm doing the girls any good here. I even thought of marrying to get them a mother, so I could go back and get myself killed. But no respectable female would have me, with my name as black as mud."

"Not with the army, sir. Why, you're one of the heroes of the Peninsula, Major. I 'spect that's because you'd go back to all that mud and heat and poor grub, if you had your druthers, rather than stay here and be a nob." The sergeant's dour expression conveyed his own opinion. Lord knew he'd follow the major to hell and back, but Robb figured they'd already been to hell. "I don't see what's so bad about two country properties," he said with the familiarity of shared battlefields, "a huntin' box, the London town house, and a healthy income. Why, you could take a seat in Parliament if you wanted, sir, and get the army boys better rations.

So what if some Tulip cut us in the park? At least we don't have to go forage for food."

The major didn't throw his cane. He didn't want to scare the horses. "Stubble it, Robb. Go see what the devil is holding us up."

While his man was gone, Major Conover tried to shut out the bawdy ditties from the mail coach and the less frequent screeches from the barouche. What was so wrong with being an earl? How about dragging up all the old scandal, or not being admitted to his brother's clubs, or his nieces thinking he was so terrible, he ate children for breakfast? How about not being trained to administer those vast holdings? How about worrying about the succession? He'd do anything in his power, including giving up his commission and his career, just to keep Warebourne and the girls' inheritances safe away from Preston. Tarnation, he'd even marry the lightskirt in the barouche.

He threw his gloves as far as he could. An urchin scooped them up and ran away. Good, let someone benefit from this hellish day.

When the sergeant returned, he related a minglemangle of stunning dimensions, even by London standards. A racing phaeton, it seemed, had been tearing down the crowded road at a high rate of speed. The driver, a young cawker who was more than a little on the go, started to take the corner where an organ-grinder and his monkey were working. A dog came out of nowhere and ran between the horses' legs, barking. The spirited horses took exception, but the choice spirit at the reins lost control, so his carriage veered, into the path of an oncoming barrel wagon. The drayman pulled his brake and managed to avoid the curricle, but the barrels started rolling out the back of the wagon. Some split open on hitting the cobblestones, but others rolled merrily along. One hit a vegetable stall on the sidewalk, another exploded a newspaper delivery cart. One barrel headed for the chaise behind, which overturned, dumping out an irate cast from the Italian Opera House. The phaeton and its castaway driver, meanwhile, had continued on out of control, scattering pedestrians and other vehicles until coming to rest, sideways, alongside a poultry cart, with foreseeable results. Beggars and street urchins and nearby residents were all in the road, grabbing up the fallen bounty while shopkeepers and lorry drivers got into fistfights. The local fire brigade was called out to catch the chickens, and the Italian Opera Company decided to conduct an alfresco rehearsal. And the monkey . . .

"Oh, and the barrels were full of pickled herring. But most of the action was over when I got there," the batman concluded with regret. "They should have it cleaned up in a shake, leastways enough for us to get through. I 'spect they'll be fightin' over who pays for what for the next two years."

They eventually made their way through the scene of the devastation, holding their noses and turning down offers for fresh-killed chickens and kippers wrapped in newspapers. They had to travel slowly around the debris of wagons and carriages, slowly enough for the major to spot the black dog lying in the gutter. He pulled the curricle to the side, receiving one last vulgar imprecation from the passenger in the barouche, which now had to negotiate around them.

"What are you doin', Major? We're late as is."

"Here, take the ribbons. I'm going to see if the dog is alive."

"I 'spect they would have killed it," Robb said, indicating the knot of angry men still arguing with the Watch. "If the horses and barrels and wagon wheels didn't." He took the reins and shook his head as the officer got painfully down from the curricle and limped to the animal sprawled on its side in the filth. Conover pulled a sticky newspaper away from the dog's face and felt its chest for a heartbeat, then ran his hands over the animal's legs. He lifted its eyelids and looked in its mouth.

"Is it dead then?" Robb called.

"No, just in shock. And it's a male. He's got a broken leg, but nothing else I can find. Hand me down the carriage blanket."

"B'gorm, Major, you can't mean to take on some broke-up mutt. It's nothin' but a stray. There's a million of 'em in London."

"Stow it, Robb. Look, he's got a collar, and he's got too much meat on his ribs to be a street dog. Someone took good care of the poor chap once. Now it's our turn."

"But, Major, sir, you wasn't thinkin' of takin' the poor sod home with us, was you? For all you know, it could be mean, or have rabies. Leastways fleas."

Conover was already wrapping the dog in the throw, taking care not to jar the broken leg. "I would have died alone out in that field if those peasants hadn't taken me in. He deserves the same chance. Besides, the children might like him. We always had pets when we were growing up. At least maybe they'll understand why I didn't keep our appointment."

Robb could only shake his head while the major carefully lifted his burden to the carriage seat, then slowly climbed up. "You drive, I'll hold the dog steady," Conover said.

The batman made one more plea for sanity. "But what if he up and sticks his spoon in the wall then? How are those little tykes goin' to feel if somethin' else dies on 'em?"

The major held the dog firmly, stroking his head. With the same tone of voice the officer used to command his men to hold the ranks, to take that hill, he ordered: "He will not die."

"She's the prettiest dog I ever saw. Let's call her Beauty."

"No, I want to call her Bess, after the queen."

From the baby: "Me. Me."

"Beauty."

"I say Bess. Maybe Queenie."

"Mimi! Mimi! Mimi!"

"Ah, sweethearts, those are all good names, but the dog is a, uh, gentleman dog."

Six-year-old Genessa gave him a dirty look. "You're just saying that because you don't like girls."

"I like girls, Gen, truly I do. But the dog is a boy." The major was mopping his brow. Robb was smirking, leaning against the table in the kitchen, where the dog lay on blankets in front of the fire, his leg splinted and wrapped.

"How do you know?" Genessa challenged.

Conover mopped harder. "I just do," he said, in a voice loud enough to make Bettina, the two-year-old, start crying.

Ten-year-old Benice solemnly declared, "If Uncle Darius says he's a boy, Gen, then he must be." But she didn't sound convinced.

Genessa moved to kick her sister, but the major got in the way. "Ouch. Boy dogs are ... bigger, sweethearts, and have broader chests and—"

Genessa had already rolled the unconscious dog over. Conover hastily threw another blanket over him.

Robb cleared his throat. "Whyn't you just call him Trouble, sir?"

What they say about the evils of the big city are true. I've been dognapped.

Chapter Seven

*W*hite slavers! Press gangs! Procurers for houses of ill repute and perversion! (Miss Sonia and Blanche Carstairs had been reading their lurid novels aloud to each other.) Anatomy professors! Oriental chefs! (I had nightmares of my own.)

Instead, a man in uniform, an officer by the markings, was cleaning my coat with a dampened cloth, and telling me what a brave fellow I was. I did not feel brave; I felt like a fool. Only a nodcock would ask directions from a dancing monkey wearing a skirt.

I smelled. My head hurt and I was sleepy, and my right hind leg was broken. I was never so glad I wasn't a horse. The soldier had strong, gentle hands and a nice voice; he brought me some warm broth with bits of meat in it. If he wanted me to be brave, I would be brave.

The next time I woke up, my new friend—Major Conover, I heard him called—carried me to a walled-in garden behind the house. He helped me stand, then turned his back. An officer, and a gentleman. I noticed on the way back that he limped, too, and wondered if the same barrel had rolled over him. Later I learned he was shot in an act of heroism.

He was certainly a coward when it came to the little girls. They say, never show your fear to a wild animal. Well, children are worse. The major was afraid of hurting them, afraid of frightening them, afraid of talking to them. And oh, how they knew it! So the fool never got to know them, never got to cuddle them, never got to love them. So how could they love him back? They were turning mean, moody, or timid, as will any creature lacking affection and security. I started straightening them out while my leg healed, before I could go home.

If there was anything I knew, it was little girls. Soon I had them laughing and playing without arguing. Of course, I was wearing bonnets and taking tea with a bunch of glass-eyed dolls and giving Baby rides on my back. Worse, I had to pretend I couldn't find three giggly little girls smelling of milk and porridge when I was It, but no one from the old neighborhood would ever know, and it was all for a good cause. At night after Baby was asleep, I had two little bodies pressed against me while the major read nursery tales. So what if they were stories I'd heard suchamany times? Gen and Benice wouldn't sit in his lap yet, but they didn't mind that we crept closer to his chair every evening. Two more Little Penny Partridges and we'd be at his knees.

Major Conover was a harder bone to chew. He was too restless to stay in the house, but came home in a blacker mood if some old acquaintance snubbed him. When the children were abed he'd help me down the stairs and we'd go to the library, where there were so many books, Miss Sonia and I could have spent every rainy day from now till kingdog come. He never read out loud. The major mostly stared at the fire and poured wine from the decanter.

Sometimes when we went out to the back garden he'd throw rocks and sticks as far toward the rear wall as he could. Now, there's a cruel man, I thought at first, until I realized he didn't intend a three-legged dog to go fetch. He was just angry. I felt bad that I couldn't stay to set him to rights, but I had a job of my own to do. Miss Sonia must be worried.

I whimpered, yes I did, wanting to go home. The major asked if my leg hurt and poured me a saucer of brandy. I could stay a day or two more, I decided, recovering my strength before I had to face that London maelstrom. Meanwhile I'd see what I could do to get Major Conover's ducks in a row. Those slovenly maids, the cook who stole, the nursemaid who spent more time with the footmen than with the children, the castaway butler, they would all feel my wrath. That was the least I could do.

Miss Sonia could do more. I made the obvious connection, then rejected the thought. One and one did not always equal two; sometimes they just stayed that way, one and one. The major did not fill the bill. He was a soldier and a sir, not a my lord, so Grandmama would be unhappy. He wasn't well to pass, judging from the run-down house and his ill-fitting uniform, so Squire might object. He gambled in low kens, Blue Ruin on his breath, saying, "Blister it, what else is there to do?" He used bad language, was cow-handed with children, and smelled bad from the cigarillos he smoked. He was so used to giving orders that he'd never make a manageable, complacent sort of husband, and he'd never be a good dancer, with that limp. Miss Sonia loved to dance. He wasn't even handsome enough, with lines on his face and a scar on his cheek, and he never talked about going to the country at all, only Portugal. Besides, I didn't even know if he was honest. He hadn't given me back yet, had he? And he never smiled.

"Blackie must be ready for more exercise, girls, the way he's bothering the servants. What do you say we take him across the street to the square for a run?" Major Conover was almost trampled in answer, as his nieces ran to find mittens and have their bonnets tied. He wished some of the eagerness were for his company, not the dog's, but he was a little heartened when Benice paused, halfway out the door, and called back, "Hurry, Uncle Darius."

He followed down the steep front steps of Ware House as quickly as he could on a leg that refused to heal, his cane in one hand, the lead Robb had fashioned for the dog obviously de trop in his other. "Do not cross the—" he started to command from the marble landing, scowling that the nursemaid was nowhere in sight. Then he noted how Blackie put his body in front of the girls at the edge of the walkway, keeping them back until there was a break in the traffic. The dog was a better nanny than any he could have hired. He stopped trying to catch up.

He followed happy squeals and excited barking to the park entry, where Blackie was whining at a pieman outside the gates. Lud, the major thought, the mutt eats everything in sight. Why does he have to act like we've been starving him? The vendor was handing out meat pasties to the girls and Blackie when Conover got there, just in time to pay, he thought, reaching for his purse.

"Oh no, sir, it's that happy I am to see Fitz again." The man did accept a coin for the pie Major

Conover munched on as he followed his noisy pack. Fitz?

Hampered by his still-splinted leg, Blackie was galumphing through the gates of the square. The children skipped behind him, playing this new kind of tag. Then Blackie started dancing clumsy circles around a flower girl on one of the paths. "Aw, Fitz, y' near t' broke our 'earts, y' did, disappearin' like that," she said, tying a bunch of violets to the dog's collar. " 'Urry on 'ome now, Fitz. Poor missy's been lookin' 'igh 'n' low."

Uncertain now, the two older girls ran after the limping dog, leaving the baby in their wake.

Darius looked around for the blasted nursemaid, who was paying them no mind at all, chatting up the pieman outside the gates. He awkwardly lifted Bettina, hoping the child wouldn't start screaming. "Come on, Tina, let's go find Blackie. Or Fitz."

"Me. Me. Mimi!"

"I don't think so, sweetheart."

Blackie-Fitz made one last stop at the opposite end of the small park. He halted in front of a silver-haired figure on a bench, barked once, and wagged his tail. He waited for the old man to put down a sack of nuts, accepted a scratch behind the ears, then took off again. When Darius and Bettina reached the bench, the elderly gentleman got slowly to his feet.

"Found our Fitz, did you, Major? Good job, soldier." And he snapped a still smart salute.

The major transferred his cane and the leash to the hand holding the baby, to return the courtesy.

This time, when the big dog reached the edge of the park, he turned on Benice and Genessa, barking in their faces, showing his teeth. They were not to cross the road behind him. He dashed between a hackney and a brougham.

Benice silently put her hand into her uncle's as they waited for a break in the traffic. Gen held the trailing end of the leash. No one said anything, listening to the dog's near frantic yelps as he made his clumsy way up a wide colonnade of steps outside a mansion even bigger than Ware House.

Sonia was trailing down the stairs to join her grandmother's company for tea. She didn't want to. She had no interest in the old ladies' gossip or the younger gentlemen's flattery. She only wanted to put on her old cape and sturdy half boots and continue searching for her dog. Maybe there was a paper she hadn't sent an advertisement, or a street urchin she hadn't told about the reward. Someone had to find Fitz. They just had to.

But she'd promised her grandmother to make an effort, with the ball just a few days away now. Maisie had taken a few hasty tucks in her gown, and Bigelow had come in to use the hare's foot to bring some color to Miss Randolph's wan cheeks. She was presentable, even if she didn't shine. Sonia didn't care.

She heard the barking, but she heard Fitz barking in her dreams these days. Or someone was bringing her another emaciated, scrofulous stray for the reward. She gave them each a coin for their trouble, hoping they would feed the animal, at least, before sending it back on the unfriendly streets. She hoped someone was feeding Fitz.

The barking was getting nearer. Sonia wouldn't get her hopes up; she'd been disappointed so many times. No, she'd just open the door an inch and peek out. Marston would look down his nose at her, but the butler must be in the parlor serving tea, for only Ian stood in the hallway. Just an inch, Sonia told herself, just to be sure.

By the time the major's small, grim-faced party climbed the covered stairs to the open door, Fitz was engulfed in sprigged muslin, a cap of golden ringlets mixed with his black fur. The dog was yowling, trying to bury himself in her lap, licking her hands, her face, wriggling with joy.

"I, ah, guess there's no question he's your dog then," the major said quietly from the doorway.

The girl raised her head from the dog's back. Darius saw her reddened nose, tears streaming down her cheeks, and the most radiant smile he'd ever expected to see this side of heaven. "We'll leave you to your reunion then," he choked out, when he could breathe again. He could feel Benice's hand trembling in his—or was it his trembling in hers?

"Oh, please don't go so fast!" The girl, no, young lady was struggling to rise, encumbered as she was by ecstatic dog. The major was too burdened himself to help her, and the chuckleheaded footman was blubbering into a square of linen in the corner. At last she was on her feet, and Darius could see that her form was as lovely as her face.

"I'm sorry for enacting you such a scene, ah, Major," she said, recognizing the insignia. "We've never been apart, you see." One hand still on the dog, she fumbled for the tiniest scrap of lace to blot her eyes, eyes he could see were the color of a summer sky. Darius wondered if he was looking at this vision any less worshipfully than the dog. He tried to pay attention to her words.

"How can I ever thank you, Major? You must have taken such good care of my Fitz, for look how shiny he is. And his leg is wrapped better than a surgeon could do. Please, please do come in, sir, you and the children, and let me offer you . . ." Sonia was going to offer the reward, noting how the officer's uniform hung on his frame as though made for someone else. His face was too thin, with haggard lines, and he was leaning heavily on his cane. But the silent little girls were in crisp white pinafores, all expensive lace and fancywork smocking.

". . . Some chocolate, at least, and Cook's macaroons, so you can tell me how you found my Fitz."

Reality intruded when the major heard voices

from a room down the hall. This sweet angel didn't know who he was. She'd never invite him in, else. "No, thank you, my lady, we mustn't impose."

"Then please, may I have your direction, that I can call on your wife to show my appreciation?"

The major looked blank for an instant, then: "Oh no, these aren't my children. They are my brother's. That is, they were. Now they are my wards." Blast it, he was as tongue-tied as a raw recruit.

"Then their mother," she persisted, fully intending to bring a gift and some toys for the children.

"She's gone, too, regretfully, and I don't have a wife, ma'am, bachelor quarters, you see, so it wouldn't be at all the thing for you to call. And not necessary, I assure you."

Truly the man was exasperating! "But there must be some way I can thank you."

"Just seeing your joy was reward enough." He smiled, and Sonia realized he was not as old as she'd first supposed, not even thirty, in fact, young to have attained such a high rank. And he was quite attractive, in a rugged way, with the same dark hair and eyes as the little girls.

"Now come, children, make your curtsies," he continued.

Benice made a wobbly bow, her lower lip quivering. When she realized they were leaving, without the dog, Bettina in the major's arms started clutching his uniform collar so tightly that Conover's face turned red. She started screaming, "Blackie! Mimi!" at the top of her lungs. And Genessa jerked at his cane so the major's bad leg nearly went out from under him.

"I won't!" she shouted. "He's our dog, Uncle Darius, you said! She lost him and we found him. Make her give him back, Uncle Darius, now."

Some of the guests in the drawing room decided to make their departures, timely enough to satisfy their curiosity as to the commotion in the hall.

"Look, Lord Berke," Sonia addressed the baron,

"Fitz has come home! These kind young ladies and their wonderful uncle just brought him." She laughed. "And I was so excited to see Fitz, I never even got their names, to make introductions."

"Just as well, Miss Randolph." Lord Berke had drawn himself up to his full height, not quite that of the officer. He raised his quizzing glass and surveyed the untidy, fractious group. One side of his lip lifted in a sneer. "He's no one anyone with taste wants to acknowledge."

Sonia gasped. She had never seen such rudeness from the baron.

"It's true, my dear, everyone knows his reputation. I am just surprised swine like that has the nerve to cross your doorway."

The major grabbed the back of Gen's dress before she could go kick Ansel Berke. What could Darius say in front of a young lady, especially one whose eyes, so recently shining with innocent tears, were now filled with shock and horror? What could he say with Baby's hands closing his windpipe? He made his bow, such as it was, to Lady Atterbury where she stood in the hall, her lips gathered in a tight O of disapproval. Then he bowed again to the young woman. "Your servant, Miss Randolph." He hauled Gen and Baby awkwardly down the stairs, Benice carrying his cane and sobbing behind them.

They didn't move fast enough to miss hearing Lady Atterbury's instructions to her butler before the door was closed: "Marston, we are not at home to Major Conover. Or Lord Warebourne. Whatever the scoundrel chooses to call himself."

A dog with a bad reputation is given a wide berth. Or shot.

Chapter Eight

Some things are better left unknown. Like the meaning behind the expression "It's a dog-eat-dog world." We know such things exist, but we do not have to speak of them, no more than we would explain the origin of "hangdog look," at least not in polite company. Shame, either personal or collective, does not need to be aired in public. For once, I agreed with Lady Atterbury when she commanded Miss Sonia to have nothing more to do with Major Conover–Lord Warebourne, and then refused to say why. "The details are too sordid for your ears," she said.

Human youngsters are forever asking why. Why can't they fly like birds, why can't they breathe underwater like fish? How in a badger's backside can anyone answer that? Why must they stay away from silver-tongued strangers with shady backgrounds?

The answer is usually "Because I say so."

This answer seldom satisfies anyone.

Every fox cub ever born has been told not to

look under a hedgehog's skirts, and every fox cub ever born has had a swollen snoutful of prickles. Forbid a lass to step out with a rake and a rogue, she'll elope. It's been that way since men started falling off the edges of the earth, looking for the unknown. Danger, forbidden fruit. Think of Eve. Everyone blames the snake—they aren't my favorites either, right down there with tapeworms—but Eve was just young. Curious and contrary and a bad dresser.

Anyway, Miss Sonia always did have a soft spot for the underdog.

"Suffice it to say, Sonia, I would not be doing right by you or the Harkness name if I permitted you near a blackguard like Darius Conover. Or Warebourne, though he shames the title."

"But, Grandmama, I am sure I have read his name in the dispatches. He is one of our own brave soldiers. Surely he deserves better than this Turkish treatment. And he took care of Fitz and brought him home. I am in his debt, Your Grace, and cannot dismiss him so cavalierly."

"Write him a letter," the dowager snapped, rapping Sonia's fingers with a teaspoon. "Then have nothing more to do with the knave, do you hear me, missy? That is all I am going to say on the subject. Drink your tea."

So Sonia asked Blanche.

"The new Lord Warebourne?" Blanche asked, her eyes wide. They were pretty hazel eyes, when she took them out of a book. The two girls were best of friends now, and Blanche had lost most of the gruff cover to her shyness. They were on their way back from Hatchard's when Sonia startled her companion with the question. "However did you get to meet him? He's not accepted anywhere."

"I know he's scorned by society; what I want to

know is why. As for meeting him, he brought Fitz home. He seemed sad and tired and overburdened with cares. I'd like to help him."

Blanche shook her head. "But, Sonia, he's not a pigeon with a broken wing or a kitchen maid needing your encouragement to see the tooth drawer. I don't think there's anything you can do, except make mice-feet of your own reputation."

Sonia's chin rose. "If you don't tell me, I'll ask the servants."

Blanche shrugged. "The original scandal happened years ago, at least five or six. Everything would have blown over by now, except that the girl he ruined was well placed, and he came back from the wars." Blanche could feel Sonia's impatience, so she got more specific. "The girl was Ansel Berke's sister Hermione. Lady Rosellen's sister, too, of course, although I think she was not long married to Conare at the time. Anyway, Hermione was found to be breeding, and she claimed Darius Conover was the father. Darius denied responsibility and refused to marry the chit."

"Perhaps he wasn't the father?"

"Who's to say? But the whole coil could have been kept quiet if he had married the girl anyway. Or if Berke had just sent her off to Ireland to have the babe. Instead Berke challenged Conover to a duel, so naturally Hermione's name became a byword. Again, things might have been settled if Darius took the usual path, but he didn't. He would not accept Berke's challenge, saying the chit wasn't worth dying for, or fleeing the country for if he killed Berke, or losing his commission over. Conover had just signed up, I think, and Sir Arthur was very strict about his officers not dueling."

"That sounds very intelligent. Dueling is barbaric."

"Yes, but Berke didn't see it that way. He'd thought to force Darius to marry Hermione one way or t'other. So he called Conover a coward, and still

72

Darius would not fight. Ansel Berke convinced everyone that Conover acted without honor. You have to know the store men set on honor, so Darius was cut. At first his brother Milo kept the worst of it away. He was the Earl of Warebourne, after all, but then his wife was breeding and he stayed in the country. And then Hermione killed herself."

"Oh my. The poor young woman."

"And Conover's hopes of being received in London were destroyed with her. They say he threw himself into the Peninsular Campaign to try to regain his honor, volunteering for hazardous assignments, making daredevil rescues."

"Surely that must have proved he was no coward, at least."

"I daresay it did. That would have turned the tide, too, especially after Milo Warebourne and his wife, Suzannah, were both lost in a carriage accident without leaving an heir. An eligible, wealthy earl can be excused many a youthful indiscretion."

"Except?"

"Except Berke would not let the matter rest. Nor would his other sister, Rosellen, whose husband, Preston Conover, Lord Conare, is incidentally next in line to the earldom. I think Lord Conare would not be upset if Warebourne is convinced to return to the perils of war. Conare has Prinny's ear, and Rosellen the Almack's hostesses', so your major's case is next to hopeless. Forget him."

"But what about the children? I should think Lady Rosellen would want Lord Warebourne received if only for their sakes. What will happen to them if they can never take their places in society?"

"What has that to do with Rosellen? Haven't you seen she cares for nobody but herself?"

Sonia nodded, dreading the time she would be consigned to the arctic lady's chaperonage.

"There's another thing," Blanche recalled, "and it's about the children. When Darius came home on injury leave, he stopped at Conare's place in Sussex to visit with his nieces. Neither Preston nor Rosellen were there, naturally, since they are always in London or Bath or at some house party. Darius scooped the little girls right out from under their care, saying they weren't taking proper charge of the children."

"Good for him!" Sonia exclaimed. "And much better for the children. Just think, leaving those dear little girls for the servants to raise!"

Blanche frowned. That's how *she* was raised. "Anyway, Lady Conare took it as an insult. I heard her saying so to your grandmother. They are thinking of petitioning the Crown to have themselves named as guardian instead of Warebourne, on grounds that he is not morally fit."

"That's outrageous. Why, anyone could see he loves those children." Actually, Sonia had seen right away that he knew as much about little girls as she knew about steam engines, but she, at least, was willing to give him credit for trying. "And as you say, Rosellen cannot claim affection for the children."

"No, but the Warebournes left a vast, unentailed inheritance to their children. Whoever gets them as wards gets to control that money for a long time. So you see, there is every reason to keep Darius Conover discredited."

"I see that the so-called polite world is an evil place of manipulation, greed, and ambition. Why, one man's life is being ruined for a crime he might never have committed, and three little girls will be ostracized for no wrongdoing of their own at all!" Sonia stamped her foot. "Well, I don't care. They were good to Fitz, and now I have to repay the kindness. That's how *I* was raised. I shall stand their friend."

Blanche almost dropped her books. "Don't be a ninnyhammer, Sonia. You'll be ruined. And you can't have thought; you're so good, you think there's good in everyone. What if he really is a cad?"

"What if he isn't? You cannot expect me to take the word of Rosellen. I'll have to know Lord Warebourne better to decide for myself. I certainly owe him that much."

Blanche sighed with relief. "That's fine then. He'll never be invited to ton affairs, so you'll never see him again. And not even you would think of calling on him at home. Would you, Sonia?"

"Of course not, goose." But there was nothing to stop her from walking her dog in the park.

Fancy that, Sonia thought after one simple inquiry, Ware House was just across the square from Lady Atterbury's. She might have seen the Warebourne children in the park any number of times, if she'd been looking. Now that she was, she decided to leave nothing to chance. She sent her footman, Ian, over to find out when the girls were usually taken for a walk. She met them and their nursemaid at the gate closest to Ware House.

The nursemaid had no fault to find with Sonia's taking the children off. The brats finally stopped whining and moping when they saw the dog; Miss Randolph was obviously a lady; and that handsome red-haired footman had a fine line of Irish blarney that fair turned a girl's head. Besides, her employer would never know. The major had not come out of his library since bringing the children home yesterday without the dog. A fine job that'd been, too, trying to stop all the crying and screaming so she could get some rest before her evening engagement with the head groom. Some fine lady wanted to play with Meg Bint's charges, she had Meg's blessings.

At first the girls were uncertain of Sonia, considering the scene at her house yesterday. Fitz's exuberant greeting quickly had them laughing and babbling like old friends, especially when Sonia

75

fetched some gingerbread from the tapestry bag at her feet and suggested they sit on the bench awhile to catch their breaths.

"There," Sonia told them, "now we can be comfortable. I was so sorry that I didn't get to thank you properly for taking care of Fitz yesterday. I didn't even catch your names. I am Miss Sonia Randolph, and this, of course, is Fitz."

Ever conscious of the proprieties, Benice stood and made a curtsy, her dignity somewhat marred by the crumbs that fell off her lap. Sonia took no notice. "We are pleased to make your acquaintance, Miss Randolph," Benice solemnly recited as if from memory. "And we are the Conover sisters of Ware House. I am the oldest, so I am Miss Conover, but you may call me Benice."

"Very prettily done," Sonia congratulated, causing the pale child to blush with pleasure.

"My middle sister is Genessa, but we call her Gen. Gen, make your curtsy!" The minx in the middle crammed the last of the gingerbread in her mouth and bobbled up and down, grinning. Sonia grinned back and handed over a napkin.

"And that's Baby. She doesn't curtsy yet. She doesn't talk much, either. She used to talk more, before . . ." The child's voice faded and her smile disappeared altogether. "Her name is Bettina. Uncle Darius says she's too old to be called Baby, so he calls her Tina. That's what our father called her." Benice's lip trembled.

"I'm sure you must miss your father ever so much. I miss mine, and he's only in Berkshire. He always called me Sunny. Do you think you might do that, so I don't feel so lonely?"

Three heads nodded somberly, then Gen asked, "What about your mother? Ours is gone to heaven with Papa."

"Mine is there, too. Maybe they'll meet and be friends, just like us. What do you think? Meantime," she said, changing the subject, "I brought you some gifts, just to say thank you from Fitz. I didn't quite know what you would like, so I hope I chose correctly." She reached into the carpetbag. "This is for you, Benice," she said, pulling out a tiny gold locket on a chain. "See, it opens. I put a snip of Fitz's hair inside—from his tail, where he won't miss it—so you won't forget him. Of course, if you have a beau, you might put his miniature there," she teased. Genessa hooted, but Benice was smiling through her blushes, and asked if Sonia would please put it on for her. "I'll wear it always, Miss Sunny. It's beautiful."

"And, Gen, this is for you." It was a bilbo-catch toy, a wooden ball meant to be caught in the wooden cup tied to it with string. "Topping!" Gen shouted, running off to try it.

The littlest Conover was jumping up and down on the bench, yelling, "Me. Me."

Sonia laughed. "I wouldn't forget you, Tiny! Here." She pulled out a little stuffed pillow in the shape of a dog, with buttons sewn on for eyes and nose, and a ribbon around its neck for a collar. "Mimi!" the baby cooed, hugging the pillow to her.

Then Sonia had Fitz do some of his tricks, to show what a smart dog he really was, even if he did get lost and run over. Fitz sat and lay down and rolled over, he shook hands and barked and fetched. He went right at a hand signal, left at another, and concluded with his bow, head lowered between his legs. The children, and a few passersby, applauded happily.

"Can we play hide and seek?" Gen asked. "Blackie was the best finder."

So the little girls ran squealing behind trees and under benches, and Fitz and Sonia made believe they couldn't find them. Then they played blind-man's buff, with one of the napkins as blindfold, and, finally, a lively game of tag before it was time to go.

"Do you think you might come tomorrow?" Sonia

asked, and three dark heads nodded vigorously. "At the same time?" More nodding. "Maybe your uncle will join us." Three little girls shook their heads no.

"He says he doesn't want to go anywhere, only back to the army," Genessa confided.

"And he stays in the library, throwing books," Benice fretted.

"Oh dear. Perhaps he would come if you tell him that I need to consult with him about Fitz's leg. What do you think?"

They all grinned. They thought it just might work.

Tag, hide-and-go-seek . . . cat and mouse?

Chapter Nine

Sometimes I envy Tippy the turnspit. Granted, her life is narrow, lived entirely between the kitchen and Cook's bedchamber, but she is too small to face the world on her own anyway. Her responsibilities are no bigger than her short little legs. Her kind has it easy now that there are enclosed stoves, so she has two jobs. By day she has a few hours on a wheel. The scenery is boring, but she says she uses the time to compose verse. By night she is a foot warmer. How hard could that be? She has none of these anguished decisions I now face. No one's future hangs on her actions. Nowhere does she feel the Great Dane's torment, unless it's to baste or not to baste.

I am torn. I have been wrong in the past about Major Conover. He does have a title, he is well to pass, and he did not accept a reward for bringing me home when we both know I found my own way. But he is still an outcast and he still smokes. Furthermore, he throws books. A desecration!

Worse, there is an alarm going off in my head. It's clanging Cinderella, Cinderella, Cinderella. Aristocratic humans have wet nurses, so ladies don't even have to see their babies, much less care for them. Stepmothers have no bonds whatsoever, neither blood nor milk; they don't have to love their adopted children at all.

I do not think Miss Sonia could ever be an evil stepmother, but how much love is there to go around? I know I grew fond of my "Blackie's" family, but I only truly love Miss Sonia. Of course, I am a good dog; I do not expect such devotion from mere humans.

Miss Sonia was growing fond of the Warebourne girls. Wouldn't she feel guilty about loving her own children better? Worse, what if there was not enough love to share so many ways? Benice, Gen, and Tina needed so much, perhaps Miss Sonia wouldn't care about having her own babies? I could have been flattened by a barrel for nothing!

No, I dare not take a chance. 'Twas better to nip this relationship in the bud now, than have to nip a butt later. I will play with the children when we meet in the park. I will play with them so hard and so rough, we'll never be allowed near them again. They'll all thank me someday.

Sonia took an inordinate amount of time selecting an outfit to wear to go for a romp in the square with her dog and some children. Goodness, she chided herself, she wasn't trying to fix Lord Warebourne's interest or anything, she just wanted to be friends with the man. Besides, he mightn't even come. She finally selected a rose-colored walking dress with its fuller skirt and higher neck than many of her new clothes. She pinned a bunch of silk violets under the brim of her chip-straw bonnet, and tied its pink ribbons along her cheek. She took her maid along with her as well as Ian, the footman, so she broke no minor rules, on her way to break major ones. She also brought a ball, so Fitz and the girls could play on their own. She sat on a bench near the Ware House side of the little park, Fitz at her feet, and waited.

He came, following slowly behind the excited children, who immediately ran laughing and tumbling after Fitz and the ball. Darius bowed stiffly, then took a seat on Sonia's bench, as far from Miss Randolph as possible without toppling off. He did not look in her direction. To a casual observer, they would appear chance-met strangers enjoying the day. Ian stepped behind a tree with the nursemaid, Meg, but Maisie Holbrook very properly kept vigil from the next bench over, keeping Miss Randolph quite in view if not exactly in hearing, while she mended a bit of lace in her lap.

Sonia studied the major while he observed the noisy game of catch. He seemed even more careworn today than she remembered, older, harder. He sat rigidly erect, military fashion, only his injured leg angled for comfort. Sonia could feel his disapproval and wondered if she had made a mistake, asking him to come where he had no wish to be. She never meant to add to the officer's discomfort.

She was about to call to Fitz, to leave Major Conover to his solitude, when he frowned, then spoke, still without looking at her. "The dog does not seem to be in a decline, Miss Randolph. He hardly favors the leg at all."

Sonia looked to where Fitz was barking and jumping, chasing the ball. "No, sir, and I am sorry the children told you such a bouncer. I did want to thank you properly for saving him, however, and to apologize for that scene at Atterbury House."

"No need, I am sure." He cleared his throat. "Miss Randolph, I appreciate your attention to the children. They are in alt over their new friends. I don't know which impressed them more, your kindness or Fitz's repertoire of tricks. Now they won't be so miserable until I can find them a puppy of their own. Or a kitten. There is some disagreement among the ranks, so the decision is still pending. I do thank you, ma'am, but this"—holding his hands out to encompass the park, the bench, his own presence—"was not well done of you. You must be aware by now that I am not fit to be in your company. I heard your own grandmother make that plain."

Sonia raised her chin. "I make my own friends."

"You are very young and foolish, then."

"I am eighteen, and old enough to know when someone has done me a great service. Fitz means the world to me, you see."

"He is a lucky dog to win such affection." He stood to leave. "Still, I cannot let you—"

"Please, don't go yet," she pleaded. "At least tell me how you found Fitz. The children's tale was all full of brave derring-do, mixed in with monkeys and schoolboys and opera singers. That sounds like quite a bumblebroth, even for Fitz."

Darius could not resist the appeal in her voice. He made the mistake of turning to her. Deuce take it, he knew he shouldn't look at those blue eyes, or catch a hint of those adorable dimples. Or note how the pink ribbons of her bonnet brought up the tinge in her velvet cheeks. And those silly violets nestled in gold curls. Gads, he loved violets. He was lost. He'd tell her about the dog's addlepated exploits, then he'd leave. For good.

The telling of the story, the vegetables, the herring, the scattered newspapers, softened the major's features and even brought a twinkle to his brown eyes. Sonia was pleased to see the years and worries slip away. She was also happy to have her own instincts confirmed: He was a good man. Sonia couldn't begin to imagine Lord Berke or any of his friends stopping for a half-dead dog, much less soiling his hands to help the filthy animal.

"I truly am in your debt," she said.

"No, I think I am in yours." Darius smiled and gestured to where Fitz and his nieces were frolicking. The ball long lost, the dog and the girls seemed to be taking turns rolling in a mud puddle. Then they went wading in the decorative fountain, splashing water on an irate matron with a beady-eyed mink tippet draped about her neck. Next Fitz took Baby on a ride through the public flower beds, scattering blossoms for the older girls to make into neck chains and hair wreaths. "I have never seen them so happy."

"And I have never seen Fitz behave so badly. Goodness, he knows he's not supposed to go near the fountains or the gardens. I'm sorry about the little girls' clothes, Major. I don't know what's got into Fitz these days. Perhaps it's spring fever. I'll just whistle him back before someone calls the Watch." Fitz was now digging a hole in the soft dirt with his powerful front legs, spraying debris on the girls and a clerk who hurried past, cursing. Benice found a stick and came to help dig. Gen and Tina just used their hands.

"No, leave them. I've never seen the girls act so . . . childishly. Especially Benice. They don't laugh enough." Just then Fitz turned and nosed Baby right into the hole. Darius laughed out loud at the stunned expression on the little girl's face.

"Nor do you, I think," Sonia murmured. She hadn't meant him to hear, and blushed when he turned back to her.

"Miss Randolph, you are very kind. Your compassion does you credit, but you mustn't let your tender heart lead you astray. For your own sake, I must go. I can see you have a strong will under that sweetness, but you must not exercise it on my behalf. I am not a charity case." He spoke gently, to discourage her, not to insult the enchanting young miss. "Truly I do not need your sympathy."

Sonia stared at the reticule in her lap. "I had hoped to enlist yours." She untied the strings and withdrew a white envelope and handed it to him. "Tomorrow night is my come-out ball. I wish you would come."

Darius looked at the envelope and read his name neatly inscribed, Major Darius Conover, Lord Warebourne. He laughed harshly. "Haven't you heard anything I said, Miss Randolph? Not even the title will keep me from being tossed on my ear."

"Not at my ball, my lord, not if I invite you myself. I am acquainted with so few people, you see, I should like to have someone familiar there. Everyone else will be Grandmother's friends."

"Deuce take it, my girl, you'll know fewer and fewer if I sit in your pocket. You'll be cut by them all."

Her lips formed a determined line. "I am not asking you to sit in my pocket, my lord, just to stand my friend. One dance is all I wish."

He gave that same humorless laugh. "I cannot even dance, Miss Randolph, with this blasted leg. A fine figure of fun that would make of us, were I to try and fall on my face in front of you and half the ton."

"I am not permitted the waltz yet, so I shall not be dancing every dance, even if I am asked."

"Even if you are asked? Are you fishing for compliments, Miss Randolph? You are beautiful, charming, and well dowered. There will be bucks and beaux lined up along the sidewalks of Grosvenor Square just waiting to ask you!"

Sonia's face was as pink as the ribbons on her bonnet. "I never meant to be so forward, my lord, truly I did not. I just do not know many of those . . . bucks and beaux, and thought I might be more comfortable sitting out a waltz with someone I know. I'm sorry. It was very improper of me to ask."

"Miss Randolph, your being here in the park with me is improper, and you dashed well know it. Your handing me an invitation your guardian didn't issue is deucedly irregular. Asking a gentleman, and

I use the term loosely, for a dance would set you beyond the pale. I am beginning to think there is the heart of a hoyden under that demure exterior," he said sternly, until he caught the beginnings of her dimples. "Are you really comfortable sitting with me?"

She nodded.

"Every other respectable female goes off in a swoon if I half nod in her direction. Why aren't you afraid?"

She countered his question with one of her own: "Do I have any reason to be afraid?"

"Beyond fearing to be tarred with the same brush? No, Miss Randolph, you never need to be afraid of me. Never."

"There. I knew Fitz wouldn't befriend a bounder." She called for the dog and turned to leave, kissing the muddy children and giving Darius one last brilliant smile. "Will you at least please consider the invitation?"

He nodded. That was all he could do, considering Miss Randolph's smile turned his brain to mush.

Darius did contemplate the invitation as he carried two exhausted, grimy children home. Blister it, where was that wretched nursemaid anyway? Benice could hardly drag his cane, while he suffered along with both Gen and Tina in his arms. Gen was smiling at him, which was worth a walk to the Isle of Wight. He knew he had Miss Randolph to thank for that, and again considered the engraved card. He thought about the ball, picturing Miss Randolph twirling in some lucky devil's arms, laughing up into some fortunate chap's eyes. Then he thought what a wretched mull he'd made of his life. Heaven seemed to be waiting just out of reach behind a locked door, and everyone but Darius Conover had the key.

* * *

Sonia and Fitz, his tongue hanging out of his mouth, made two stops on her way out of the park. First she checked with the flower girl to make sure lots of violets were on order for the ball. Most of the flowers and greenery for the formal arrangements were coming from Lady Atterbury's favorite florist, but Sonia saw no reason her friends shouldn't profit from the party, too. The pieman was already providing a quantity of gooseberry tarts to augment the Atterbury kitchens.

Sonia's last stop was by the bench of the silver-haired man feeding the squirrels, where she sat down before the elderly gentleman could struggle to his feet. Fitz sank to the ground next to them. A squirrel ran right over the snoring dog, and he didn't move. Sonia took another card out of her reticule and handed it to the old man.

"I already got one, missy," he rasped.

"I know, and I already got your refusal. I am hoping you'll reconsider and accept this one." She proceeded to tell him why. He shook his head no. She teased and cajoled until he nodded yes, then she kissed his cheek and went home humming a waltz.

So much for the best-laid plans of mice and mongrels.

Chapter Ten

$\mathcal{T}$onight I stand guard like Cerberus, watchdog of the underworld. I wish I had three heads like mighty Cerberus, to keep better vigil at the ball. Marston, the butler, defends the front entry against indignity, calling off the guests' names and honorifics with resonant cadences. I have been assigned the rear garden. I was told, "Fitz, you stay outside tonight." That is a lot of responsibility. I patrol the yard to make sure no intruders come over the walls. I watch the lantern-lighted paths to guarantee no young couples go beyond the line. I pace the balcony outside the ballroom to keep rakes from taking advantage of the darkness and a miss needing fresh air. Mostly I try to keep sight of Miss Sonia as she dances and strolls about, meeting this handsome youth, smiling at that likely lad, granting a quadrille to a paragon in puce satin.

I wish Muffy were here. She could imitate a wig and sit atop one of the footmen's heads and guard the refreshments. Tippy assures me there are always leftovers, but this is my first London ball. I admit I am nervous.

I am not apprehensive that Miss Sonia will not "take." She has been considered an Incomparable since the receiving line. From the drawing room window I hear Miss Sonia discussed in glowing terms, thank St. Francis. She is described as no niminy-piminy girl, but not too coming either. She has fresh charm, not airs and affectations. She is just right, and her dowry is nothing to sneeze at either. We are a success. I am worried, however, that *she* will be taken with the wrong man. Lady Atterbury says that the crème de la crème of society is here tonight. What if its dregs arrive, too?

I wonder if he will come, this lord who would be a soldier. If he likes Miss Sonia, he will come, because he wants to be with her and because she asked. If he likes her, though, he won't come, lest he hurt her chances and disturb Lady Atterbury. More complications. Sometimes I think my life would be easier if they were like trout, the females laying their eggs in one place and the males coming there to leave a token of their affection before going about their own business.

Major Conover or not, tonight is a turning point. I can feel it in my belly. Maybe that's the wine I tasted with Ian earlier, just to make sure it hadn't turned. But Miss Sonia's beau ideal might be here tonight. He might be kissing her fingertips this very minute, while I make fog-breath on the glass doors. Rats!

Still, I am curious about this diversion they call a ball, a toy, a plaything. I am trying to understand what they find so entertaining about cramming four hundred people in space for three, standing on line for hours to shake someone's hand, having their feet trod upon, their names vilified behind their backs, and their heads muddled with champagne. They gamble beyond their means, and they dance like performing bears.

At first the men are in groups on one side of the room, and the women on the other. Then some of the braver lads ask the most well-favored lasses for the set. Lady Atterbury and her friends go around forcing other gentlemen to take the floor, but some of them escape to the card room or the balcony to blow a cloud—incidentally obscuring my view. Some of the girls are therefore left without partners, so they take up positions around the perimeter and pretend they are just another flower arrangement.

When the music begins, the dancers all follow the same patterns and movements. Everyone to the right, everyone to the left, as if they are being herded by a Chopin-loving collie. The waltz is different, but of course, the young ladies, the ones in whose honor the ball is thrown, cannot take part. They sit and watch their older sisters and widowed aunts snabble the most dashing bachelors while they are left with sputtering striplings.

I am intrigued to see the elite at play. Are they having fun yet?

Lady Atterbury was pleased. Not even Sally Jersey or those other rattlepates from Almack's could find fault tonight. Every surface of Atterbury House gleamed, the staff was superbly and unobtrusively efficient, the refreshments extravagant. The dowager had expected no less.

At first she was annoyed with the floral arrangements, banks of daisies and ferns in the ballroom, baskets of violets on each table in the supper room. Common, the dowager decided, wrinkling her patrician nose. And just like her goosecap of a granddaughter, flaunting her humble country origins.

Lady Almeria sent upstairs for another diamond brooch to join the three she already wore, next to the ruby and diamond parure, the blinding tiara, and the eight rings. Heaven forfend anyone mistake the household of Her Grace, the Duchess of Atterbury, for a woodland meadow. Then various matrons came to compliment the dowager on how cleverly the decorations reflected her granddaughter's fresh charm. Just the right touch, Princess Lieven enthused, for a miss not yet jaded by the Season. A joy to see a gel bright as a daisy, Emily Cowper congratulated, so sweetly friendly and lively, not like one of London's delicate hothouse blooms. Lady Atterbury commended herself on her excellent taste and grasp of the social niceties. She also graciously accepted credit for her granddaughter's appearance. Yes, the chit did the Harkness name proud tonight.

Madame Celeste had done the impossible: created a white gown that wasn't white. The slip of a satin undress was white, but the skirt, which began right under a minuscule bodice, was covered with three layers of tissue-thin net in three shades of blue. The gauzy mesh floated at Miss Randolph's feet, changing colors to reflect the dancing lights in her blue eyes. The white bodice was embroidered all over with forget-me-nots, the center of each flower a pearl. Sonia wore Lady Atterbury's gift of pearls and, in her fair curls, a sapphire butterfly sent by her father for the occasion. George had sent the matching earbobs, and her younger brother, Hugh, arriving barely in time for the dinner before the ball, brought her a gold filigree fan.

"Bang up to the nines, Sunny," he told her approvingly as he led her out for the first dance. "Never thought you'd hold a candle to Catherine, but demmed if I didn't have my blunt on the wrong filly. Your dance card is already filled, and you have the blades lined up two-deep to fetch you a lemonade. By George if you ain't a success. Little Sunny with her dirty face and skinned knees and mare's-nest hairdos. Who'd have thought it?"

Sonia chuckled. "Thank you, I think. I just wish Papa was here to see it."

Hugh looked quickly to make sure she wasn't getting weepy on him. No, Sunny was a Trojan. "He'd just grumble about the expense and disappear into the card room anyway. Then he'd brag to everyone for days how you looked fine as five-pence."

"In case I didn't mention it earlier, you are looking very fine yourself, Lieutenant, in your handsome new dress uniform. In fact, I can see the hopeful mamas ringing Grandmother now, waiting for their chances."

Hugh missed his step and nearly trod on Sonia's toes. "Sorry, but hang it, Sunny, I ain't going to dance with every fubsy-faced chit in the place. Just because Pa got himself leg-shackled and George is under the cat's-paw don't mean I have to do the pretty all night. I'm no hand at this blasted dancing anyway. Now, put me on the parade grounds . . ."

"Just one dance, Hugh, with one particular friend of mine, Lady Blanche Carstairs. She hasn't many partners yet, and I do not want her to be unhappy at my ball. Besides, you'll like her. She's a good listener."

Sonia was pleased, later, to see Hugh return from the card room to escort Blanche down to supper. She herself went down with Ansel Berke, as earlier arranged. She laughed, she flirted, she was having a wonderful time at her own ball. Sonia made friends with the other debutantes, happily distributing her leftover suitors among them for the remaining dances. She met so many charming gentlemen, she couldn't keep their names straight, although Lord Wolversham impressed her with his knowledge of farms and crops and sheep. She sat out one of the waltzes with the good-looking marquess, listening raptly, sending more than one gentleman hurrying to change his bets at White's.

Not till long after the supper dance did Miss Randolph betray the least nervousness, and then only by frequent glances toward the ballroom door. No one else noticed her distraction, she hoped, as she fluttered her fan and discussed the weather and the king's health with her latest partner.

He wasn't going. He was in his dress uniform, hastily tailored to compensate for the weight loss from his injury, but he wasn't going. The formal sword lay polished in his hand, ready to be strapped to his hips, but Major Conover was not going to buckle it on. He'd sooner walk through the French lines than walk across Grosvenor Square to Atterbury House. A carriage would save his leg, but get him there sooner. No, he put the sword down. Again. His batman, Robb, was like to skewer him with it if he didn't decide soon. "Deuce take it!" Darius stormed. Robb hurried to remove the sword from the major's reach. Then they heard the pounding at the door.

"Who the devil could that be? Dash it, no one calls for weeks, then someone comes banging in the middle of the night when I am trying to dress. We've been so long without guests in this wretched place, the blasted servants have forgotten whose job it is to open the door. Go get rid of whoever it is, Robby, while I try to make my mind up."

Robb was happy to get out of the way of his employer's impatience. Damned if the major didn't need a good fight to settle him down, he thought. Prebattle jitters, that's what ailed the man. Robb nodded sagely on his way to get the front door. He returned a few minutes later, pale and shaken.

"Well, what was it, Sergeant, a lost traveler or some accident in the square? I hope you got rid of the nuisance, whatever it was. I'm in no mood to—"

"Admiral Cathcart, sir" was all poor Robb could utter.

"What's that, Robb?" The major was recombing his newly trimmed hair, for the fourth time. He was wondering if the gray showed less, now that his hair was in the shorter style currently in favor. "I thought you said Admiral Cathcart. Old fellow must be dead these ten years or so."

"Downstairs, sir. He's downstairs!"

"Admiral Cathcart, who fought with Nelson? Who won so many commendations, they had to make up new ones? Good grief, what's he doing alive? No, I mean what's he doing here?"

"I left him having sherry in the drawing room, Major, but I don't think you should keep him waiting, sir."

"By Jove, I should think not." He snatched up the dress sword and buckled it on as he raced down the stairs. "Admiral Cathcart, in my drawing room."

The elderly man in the drawing room was blinding in his gold braid. He had enough ribbons on his chest to open a shop. Major Conover knew he had never met the silver-haired admiral before, but he had saluted him once. He gazed admiringly at one of the nation's greatest heroes, an old man who fed squirrels in the park.

"Sir, this is a great honor, but . . ."

"Come to request your escort, young man. Told a lady I'd honor her ball. Don't get out much, though, don't want to make my big appearance lookin' like a dodderin' old fool, leanin' on some pesky civilian footman. Spoil the effect, don't you know. The lady suggested you. Fellow officer and all, even if you're not a navy man."

"So you want me . . . ?" He looked at the cane in his hand, then laughed. "I am not so steady on my pins, Admiral Cathcart. I think the lady was just using every weapon in the arsenal."

"Aye, bringin' out the heavy artillery. Good tactician, that girl, don't take no for an answer. She seems to want you at her ball. I aim to get you there, short of callin' out the militia. Can't tell you how the chit brightens my day. Least I can do, then."

"But, Admiral, sir, you can't know—"

"I still have my oars in the water, lad. I know it's no easy thing she's askin', but just one dance. You've faced worse."

"Have I, sir?" Put like that, no self-respecting soldier could refuse. The credit of the regiment, the regard of this venerable old seadog, his own honor, were at stake. "You don't leave me much choice."

"Never meant to, soldier. Never asked more of a man than I thought he could give, either. Don't disappoint me. And don't disappoint that little girl's trust either, or I'll have you blown clear out of the waters."

Marston, the butler, did not know whether to filch another bottle of His Grace's port, or just start packing. The ball had been declared a sad crush, which is to say a great success, and then disaster struck. An appearance by the reclusive Admiral Cathcart would be the coup of the season. An appearance by the reprehensible Major Conover would be the end of Marston's career. But the fellow had an invite, in miss's own hand, and the admiral was leaning on the major's shoulder, waiting to be announced. Marston took a deep breath. In loud, ringing tones, he called out the admiral's name and honorifics. Everyone gasped and turned toward the door. In not so loud, barely tinkling tones, Marston announced Major Darius Conover, the Earl of Warebourne. Everyone gasped again. Not another word was said. The orchestra was not even playing, between sets as it was. The crowd on the dance floor parted as the two militarily erect men, neither bowed by age or adversity, made their slow, careful way across the room to where Lady Atterbury held court on a sofa, Miss Randolph by her side.

The general bowed to Lady Atterbury, then turned and made her a formal introduction to "one of our fine, brave lads."

Lady Atterbury could only smile and nod. Sonia made her curtsy, then relinquished her seat next to the dowager to Admiral Cathcart, with a wink. Two chairs appeared alongside, and Sonia gestured to one. "Will you join me for the waltz, sir?" At the major's nod, she gestured to her footman, who signaled the orchestra. A waltz was instantly begun, to the consternation of those who had reserved a *contredanse*. When Sonia's court had departed to find their own partners, Darius finally took his seat beside her.

"Do you always get your way, minx?" he asked, motioning toward the admiral.

She flashed her dimples. "Was it so terrible?"

"Like walking the world's longest gangplank," he said with a laugh, then fell silent, looking at her.

Color rose in Sonia's cheeks, and in the expanse of white skin left exposed by the narrow bodice. "Major, you are staring," she whispered from behind her fan.

"I am trying to memorize your dress and such so I can describe you to the brats tomorrow. I think I'll just tell them to imagine a fairy princess floating on sunbeams over sky blue lakes."

"How lovely! I didn't know you military men had such poetical turns, Major."

He looked at her and smiled. "Neither did I."

Sonia was relieved to see him smile. He wasn't mad, he wasn't miserable. He was, in fact, so handsome when he smiled, she half hoped none of the other girls saw it. But that was part of her plan, so she made every effort to keep him smiling, telling about Fitz's exploits, asking about his nieces, describing her hey-go-mad brother's latest effort at gaining preferment. He told about his own childhood pets and some of his milder army pranks. She thought she'd gladly trade all the night's compliments for one of his laughs.

Soon the dance was ended and Miss Randolph's next partner hesitantly approached to claim her. The major rose and bowed over Sonia's hand, then brought her hand to his lips. He did not say anything, but he squeezed her fingers, and held them a fraction longer than strictly proper.

I believe that is called putting the cat among the pigeons.

Chapter Eleven

They say elephants have long memories. Mankind better hope the immense creatures don't also hold grudges. Imagine such large, long-lived beasts being persecuted for keyboards, dice, fans, and hairpins. That should be enough to make anyone cross as crabs. Crabs as big as cottages. I hope to have a coze with the elephants at the Tower Menagerie someday.

Human memories, by contrast, are as fickle as fleas, like tonight at the ball, when the doyennes seated inside recall that they always considered Darius Conover more dashing than his brother Milo, even if he was a bit of a rake. A bit of a rake? Half an hour ago he was a debaucher of women! The gentlemen in the book room are re-telling war stories, with the major featured as the bravest man in the British army, when yes-terday he was too cowardly to accept a duel. And the young females who last week shivered in fright if he passed them on the street, tonight shiver in delight if his eye catches theirs.

Are their loyalties as inconsistent as their

memories? If Baron Berke and his sister Rosellen do not forget about their dead, dishonored sister, will their friends and the rest of the ton forget the major's role? Their loyalties seem to be king, God, and country, with expediency a close fourth. And the king is all about in his head.

Consider Lord Felton making a liaison with Sir Norbert's wife on the balcony right now, while Sir Norbert is enjoying the favors of Mrs. Quentin-Jones in the curtained alcove next to the library. Perhaps they temporarily forgot their marriage vows. Or perhaps they change their loyalties as often as their outfits.

Sirius, I am not expecting human persons to be as faithful as dogs. That would be like barking at the moon. Just ask Odysseus. His wife may have stayed true all those years, unpicking her weaving and all, but she didn't even recognize the poor sod when he finally got home. Nor did his son, his friends, his servants—only noble Argos, his old dog. That's loyalty. That's a good dog, Fido.

I do not think Miss Sonia will be inconsistent once she gives her affection. She loves me forever, of course, but she has never forgotten her old friends either, or given up on an idea she believes in. Perhaps I am premature; the Dog Star knows I've been wrong before. Possibly Miss Sonia is just repaying a debt, and maybe she will consider her job done, now that she has brought the major back into the fold. His staying there will be up to him and the rest of the sheep, ah, society. I cannot tell from here, blast it! I cannot even tell if there are any lobster patties left.

Admiral Cathcart and the major stayed through one more dance, the admiral remaining seated on the couch next to Lady Atterbury. Major Conover might have left, but the admiral signaled for the officer to take a position beside him, guarding the flank. Leaning slightly on the sofa back, Darius did not intrude on the conversations, but anyone wishing to shake hands with the admiral perforce had to shake Conover's hand. And Lady Atterbury had to make the introductions. She looked as if she had an oyster stuck in her throat, and someone had just reminded her it was alive.

Many of the company wished to greet one of the great heroes of Trafalgar, to proffer an invitation or mention a promising nephew in the navy. With a nod or a gesture Darius made sure the old gentleman had wine to drink and space to breathe and pauses between introductions. He was the one to note when the admiral's voice faltered, and laughingly suggested they retire to fight another day. Even Lady Atterbury had to commend his solicitous regard for the admiral, although it rubbed against the grain. She went so far as to offer her hand when he made his adieus.

Others noted Warebourne's kindness, his quiet dignity, and chiseled features—they also recalled his title and fortune—and began to reconsider their long-held positions. No one could doubt his bravery, not with a chestful of medals and the admiral's patent endorsement. Nor could they question his conduct. For tonight, at least, he had been all that was proper, charming the little Harkness heiress without enticing her to the balcony, the alcoves, or the primrose path. No one was ready to rush home to send him a bid for a card party or to request his presence at their daughter's come-out, but they were thinking it mightn't be such a bad idea to acknowledge a young, handsome, wealthy earl. As for the rest, the jury was still out. The haut monde would wait to see Lord Conare and Baron Berke's reaction to Warebourne's reentry into society before issuing a verdict or an invite.

* * *

Lord Conare and Baron Berke were presently in the rear garden. Their reactions, if anyone could have seen them, were at best anger and disgust. At worst, vicious fury and violent loathing. They both took care that the polite world never saw such raging emotions. That wasn't good ton.

Preston Conover, Lord Conare, was as tall as his cousin Darius, with the same dark hair and brown eyes. Unlike the soldier's well-muscled body, however, Conare's frame was thin to the point of emaciation. His indoor pallor and fashionable but somber clothes, all black and white without a hint of color, made him appear even more cadaverous. His hair was never out of place, he never exerted himself. He'd perfected the art of ennui to where he could take snuff, utter a set-down, and yawn at the same time. Since he could both drink and gamble to excess without apparent effect, he was a welcome member of Prinny's coterie.

Preston's austerity was the perfect foil for his wife, Rosellen's, lush beauty. Her auburn tresses, emerald eyes, bountiful curves, flamboyant dress style, and flirtatious manner captured the attention, but Preston did the behind-the-scenes social maneuvering. They made an interesting couple, invited everywhere. That's why he married her, that and her Berke and Atterbury connections. Which he was regretting more heartily every day.

Ansel Berke was not a large man, but he was as fit as most idle members of the aristocracy, working out occasionally at Gentleman Jackson's or Cribb's Parlor, riding in Hyde Park at the fashionable hour. What exercise and nature had not provided, Berke augmented with padded shoulders and nipped-in waists, which seemed to require more gaudily embroidered waistcoats and more extravagantly tied neckcloths. He wasn't quite a dandy, he told himself; he did not wear yellow Cossack trousers or soup-plate-size buttons. He might have—high-heeled slippers particularly tempted him—but he had a position to uphold.

He was a baron. He was also nearly run off his feet. Where his brother-in-law Preston was always cool and seemingly unaffected, Ansel was something of a hothead. He usually managed to keep his emotions as hidden as his financial state, for the sake of his social standing, but tonight his temper was unchecked. No one could hear him out in the garden behind Atterbury House, so far from the ballroom, and no one could see him in the faint light of the Chinese lanterns strung along the garden paths. No one, that is, except his brother-in-law Preston, who already despised Berke. The sentiment was returned.

"I thought you said the bastard would return to the wars and get himself killed if I brought up the old scandal," Berke raged. "Did you think I wanted my family name dragged through the mud again, you prig?"

Preston flicked a speck of lint off his sleeve. "In case you have forgotten, brother, Conover is my name also. Furthermore, I did marry your sister, you know. Despite the unpleasantness, I made sure all doors would stay closed to him. His pride could not let him remain in England."

"In case you haven't looked, he's inside now, cozying up to Lady Atterbury."

"Then you haven't done your job, old chap. Remember your vows of vengeance?"

"No amount of scandalmongering is going to bring Hermione back."

"No, but it might save the little heiress for you. Did you see the look on her face when he kissed her hand?"

Berke did. That's why he had to leave the ballroom before his anger erupted like a raging volcano. Sonia had never smiled at *him* that way. "Leave Miss Randolph out of this, you muckworm. I noticed the way *you* looked at her, *brother*. She might have been dessert, the way you drooled."

Preston smoothed his cuffs. "I am never so gauche

as to drool, although la Randolph is a tempting morsel. Never fear," he added when Berke started making growling noises in his throat, "I shan't hunt your covers, at least not until the vixen is caught. After the chit is married, of course . . ."

Berke would worry about that when the time came. "Well, that's not getting rid of Warebourne. Besides, there's no guarantee he'll be killed even if he does go back to the front. The devil's been lucky all these years."

Preston sighed. "I know, I know. Gunshots, innumerable saber wounds, to say nothing of infection and the various plagues that carry off most of the wounded. He's survived them all. Wearisome, isn't it? No, you'll just have to call him out."

"What?" Berke shouted. Then, quickly looking around and speaking more softly, he asked, "What do you mean, I'll have to call him out?"

"Simple, dear boy. You'll merely demand he meet you on the field of honor. You never had satisfaction, remember? You cannot swallow that and still call yourself a man."

"No more than one who lets another do his dirty work for him," Berke sneered.

"You're not suggesting I challenge Cousin Darius myself, are you? Think, Ansel, as hard as the effort might be. My motives just might be a tad suspect. You, however, have righteous indignation on your side, your family's honor to be redeemed. Popular sentiment shall be in your favor; you'll have everyone's sympathy."

"He refused before. Who's to say he'll take up the gauntlet this time?"

"By all accounts he's no coward." Preston shrugged. "If he does forfeit, he'll lose whatever acceptance this night's work has gained him. Not even that doddery old relict Cathcart will take his arm. No visits to Atterbury House, no playing the hero for the Randolph chit. Mark my words, he'll rejoin his regiment, and I'll start praying for Bonaparte's success again."

Berke kicked a stone out of his way. "And what if he does accept the challenge? Fellow must have learned to shoot straight in all these years."

"What, dear Ansel, balking at the gate?" He looked over to the other man, where a paper lantern cast a reddish glow on the baron's already empurpled cheeks.

"I ain't no craven," Berke stormed. "I'd call you out in a minute if I thought you'd accept, you blasted mortician."

"Sorry, too, too fatiguing."

Ansel muttered something under his breath. Then, "But what if I kill him? Having Warebourne out of the way is all fine and good for you, but my chances with the Randolph girl ain't improved if I have to flee the country."

"Do I have to do all the thinking? You are a crack shot, Ansel. You don't aim to kill, for Satan's sake. You've seen the condition he's in. One more wound, another loss of blood, that should take the trick. Perhaps we might even help him along some, but not with your bullet, my dear baron. I'll guarantee Prinny won't kick up a dust. After all, if I as nearest relative don't complain, how can the Crown?"

"I still don't see why I have to be the one to force the duel," Berke complained. "I ain't the one who'll inherit the title and the fortune."

"And I'm not the one who needs to marry an heiress. Of course, there is still the Carstairs female."

Berke grimaced, but said nothing. Conare went on: "Of course, her title is older than yours. I shouldn't think a gentleman could sleep well, knowing his wife outranks him. Then again, waking to face Lady Blanche at the breakfast table . . ."

"She's not as bad as all that, especially since Miss Randolph's taken her in hand some."

"Then why haven't you offered? Why not go inside and sweep her off to the balcony, get down on your knee, and ask for her hand and fortune this very night? There's no competition, no chance she'll say no, not if she ever expects to wed, that is."

"Rosellen wants me to have the Randolph girl," Berke mumbled.

"What's that? Oh yes, dear loving Rosellen, who's agreed to bear-lead an Incomparable, just so you two will be thrown together. Imagine her chagrin if all those thousands of Atterbury pounds go to Hermione's seducer. I'm afraid she might even stop helping you with those pressing debts of yours."

"Are you holding the money over me, you bastard? It won't wash. There's always a rich Cit looking for a title. And don't keep harping on Hermione, either. You don't care about her, you never did, so don't pretend you give a rap because she was Rosellen's sister, too. You have everything to gain here, Preston, and you don't even need the blunt. You'll get control of the three Warebourne brats' fortunes at the least, and all of Warebourne at the most."

"Yes, dear boy, but what both of us, you and I, will get the most satisfaction from is ridding the world of Darius Conover."

As the two men started back toward the balcony from the garden's farthest wall, neither saw the black dog dash ahead of them between a topiary unicorn and an ornamental fountain. Neither noticed when the dog's route intersected the graveled walkway they were taking back to the ballroom, nor were they the least aware that the animal paused a moment where the hanging lanterns cast the least light.

I hope you get a lot of satisfaction from ridding your satin dancing pumps of that, you maggots.

Chapter Twelve

$\mathcal{A}$nd they say we fight like cats and dogs. I'd rather have an honest swipe at my nose than a knife in my back.

The ball wasn't over till nearly dawn, and yes, there were leftovers. Tippy had saved me a nice bone, so I agreed to peruse her poems the next morning while I gnawed. At first I was reluctant, and not just because I had weightier matters to consider, like the conversation in the garden. Commenting on a friend's work can be embarrassing. It can even cost the friendship. I did not want to hurt the little bitch's feelings or discourage art in any form, but, quite frankly, I was expecting mere doggerel.

I was happily surprised. Tippy's verses were on eternal themes, the turning cycles of the seasons, the orbits of the planets, the ultimate circle of life and death, dust to dust, ashes to ashes. Why should I have expected less from one who goes round and round half the day in a wheel? Tippy says her mentor, a mouse who used to live behind the wainscoting in the library, had advised her to write what she knew.

I suppose that is what I am doing, writing what I know, trying to write *everything* I know, in case I never get the chance again. This could not be how true novelists go about the thing, for I cannot believe Maria Edgeworth and the other ladies who write for the Minerva Press have ever been locked in dungeons, tossed from cliffs, set adrift, or sold into harems. They could hardly have time to write. No, they must have imagination, at which human persons excel.

When he couldn't reach the grapes, Reynard decided the grapes were sour; he didn't imagine sprouting wings and flying after them. Now, think of the poor dog of Icarus. The hound puts in a hard day guarding the house, warning of strangers, making sure his master is not disturbed. He looks up—and gets melted wax in his face. There is no way in hell that dog thought he had to protect Icarus from the Sun. He had no imagination; Icarus did. I admire creativity. Some have it, some don't.

Consider the flowers that are arriving all morning. The custom here in London is for gentlemen to send a token of appreciation to the ladies who honored them with a dance, especially the young lady in whose honor the ball was held. The gifts are supposed to be trifles, not personal items such as clothing, nor expensive offerings like jewelry. As a result, the footmen have been carrying in floral tributes since before breakfast. Think about it. Not five hours before, those same gentlemen saw Atterbury House filled with daisies and violets and formal arrangements. We need more flowers like an affenpinscher needs more fleas. No imagination at all.

Baron Berke's bouquet was the biggest. I suppose he sent his florist imaginary shillings. Lord Wolversham had his groom deliver a treatise on sheep dips, with his compliments. This may have been too imaginative a gift. Miss Sonia went into whoops over her chocolate.

Sir Montescue Pimford, one of the new young men from last night, sent a lovely poem. Unfortunately it was one of Byron's, according to Tippy.

Major Conover's offering was everything a gift should be for such an occasion: appealing without being extravagant, original instead of outré, sensitive. Brilliant, in fact. He sent a picture of me.

As I said, some have it, some don't.

"Whatever that man sent, Sonia, you'll have to return it." Lady Atterbury was clutching her vinaigrette. "I shall not scold anymore over the damage done last night, but I shall not countenance a further disregard for proper behavior."

Sonia held the wrapped package on her lap. "Fustian, Grandmama. If people were going to snub us because we—" she caught her grandmother's glare "—very well, *I* invited Major Conover, they would not have sent flowers. Furthermore, I shouldn't want to know anyone so stiff-rumped and prosy."

"Sonia Randolph, your language! I told Elvin he was raising you up to be a shameless baggage. He never listened. Now look, low company, cant language. You'll soon be a byword on the Town. I am too old for such a hubble-bubble." She took a restorative sip of sherry, for her nerves' sake only, of course. "Elvin has a lot to answer for, and I've a mind to send for the nodcock, wedding journey or no. At his age, it might kill him anyway. I could be doing the cod's-head a favor."

"Humbug, Your Grace, you know Father would tell me to trust my own judgment. And keep my own accounts. Besides, you loved every minute of the admiral's visit. Why, I wouldn't be surprised if he became your cicisbeo. See, you are blushing! And Sally Jersey almost tripped over Mrs. Drummond-

Burrell to meet him and invite him to her rout, so we are not sent to Coventry yet."

"Yet. And that's Admiral Cathcart, not some black sheep soldier. Conover ain't been accepted yet, missy, and might never be. That remains to be seen, and till it is, he ain't to be seen in my drawing room!"

Sonia raised her chin and looked her grandmother straight in the eye. "Then I shall meet him in the park if he asks."

Lady Atterbury clutched her heart. "Catherine was such a nice, biddable girl."

"I am not my sister." She returned to the tissue-covered parcel in her lap.

"Whatever it is, I'm sure it's unsuitable." The dowager's nostrils flared in disapproval. "What could a reprobate like that know about genteel manners? If that's jewelry, miss, he is as much a loose screw as they say. I won't stand for any havey-cavey business. Do you hear me, Sonia? No Harkness has fallen from grace yet, and I don't intend you to be the first. There will be no expensive gifts and no clandestine meetings!"

"Yes, Grandmother, I shall invite him for tea, then." She was too busy unwrapping the package to pay attention to her grandmother's moans. Under the tissue were three separate rolled papers, each tied with a ribbon.

"By Jupiter, if he's sending you the deeds to a love nest, I'll have his liver and lights!"

Sonia chuckled. "Why do you insist he has designs on my virtue? They are most likely just poems like Sir Montescue's." She sounded disappointed. Then she untied the ribbons and just said, "Oh."

"Well? What does the rake say that's got you so moonstruck?"

"He doesn't say anything. In fact, the gifts are not from him. They are from his nieces. Look."

The first scrolled page was a black smudge, as if someone had rubbed ashes into the paper. The second was a definite drawing, a black many-legged figure on a green foreground, with a tree or perhaps a building in the back. Large, messy letters across the top identified the picture: "Fitz, by Genessa Conover." The third page, though, needed no label. Benice had painstakingly colored Fitz, gold eyebrows, white bib, splinted leg, and all. He was sitting in a field of flowers, or perhaps on a Turkey carpet, and he was smiling.

Sonia searched in her pocket for a handkerchief to wipe her eyes. "This is the nicest present I've ever had."

Lady Atterbury, her own eyes suspiciously damp, just said, "Humph."

Lady Rosellen paid a morning call. Stunning in cherry-striped lutestring, she was everything gracious about the ball to Lady Atterbury. She ignored Sonia entirely, as if she were a schoolgirl permitted to take tea with her elders, or some type of upper servant.

"The darling flowers were just the right touch, Your Grace. So sweetly innocent, no one could blame Sonia for her faux pas. I mean, entertaining a man the *belle monde* turns its back on. Too, too farouche. I can only hope the Almack's hostesses are as forgiving of the child, Lady Almeria. I was so looking forward to introducing her in King Street. Now, of course, I doubt she'll get the vouchers."

"They arrived this morning, Lady Conare," Sonia was delighted to announce. "Lady Jersey's own footman delivered them first thing. She even wrote that I might attend in her party if Lady Atterbury is not up to the outing, so if you'd rather not escort such a green girl, I understand perfectly."

Lady Rosellen's eyes narrowed. She wondered how much the chit actually did understand. Did she know, for instance, how much Rosellen needed Lady Almeria's continued approval for the times her own behavior sailed a little close to the wind, or how much Rosellen's brother needed the little bird-wit's blunt? "Nonsense, my dear, of course I'll be your duenna for the evening." She gave her tinkling laughter. "Though I am scarcely old enough for the role."

Both Sonia and Lady Atterbury nodded politely, but without the reassurances Rosellen expected. She pursed her painted lips. "Perhaps I am older and wiser enough, my dear, that you'll heed my warning. Young girls cannot be too careful of their reputations, and the man is dangerous."

The man didn't look dangerous, Sonia thought, sitting as he was among Lady Atterbury and her cronies, trying to balance a delicate china teacup on his knee and fend off the circling sharks at the same time. He looked more like a minnow than a barracuda, and there was nothing Sonia could do but smile from across the room. She and Blanche had been assigned the tea cart and the pianoforte, respectively, half to keep them safe from his rakish clutches, half not to spoil the old ladies' fun.

Lady Atterbury had complained that life was wearying enough keeping fortune hunters away from her granddaughter; now she had to worry about libertines. "Lud," she said, "Catherine never even *met* one, much less brought one home to tea!" She was determined to send this thatch-gallows to the right-about. At least he'd be sure someone was looking out for Sonia's interests.

Blanche was pounding away at the instrument, looking more than passable in a new pink frock that didn't make her skin look so sallow. Sonia, in buttercup yellow, took every opportunity to refill cups, pass macaroons, and in general stand ready to toss a lifeline. So far the major was holding his head above water. He even managed to wink up at her once, when she brushed past him with a plate of almond cakes.

Darius hurriedly gathered his wits from where they'd gone begging after a sunbeam. "What's that, Lady Atterbury? I'm sorry, you were saying . . . ?"

"I was asking why you don't use the title, boy. It's a fine old name, almost as old as Atterbury. You ain't ashamed of it, are you?"

"Ashamed? Of course not. I'm just not used to it. My brother was Warebourne for the last ten years. I still look around for Milo when I hear someone call Warebourne."

"Then you're not rejecting the title because you'll bring shame to it?"

If a gentleman asked another man such a question, he'd have to name his seconds. Darius took a deep breath and contemplated the tiny teacup in his hand. He carefully placed it on the table in front of him, out of temptation's way. "I am proud of my family name," he said, "but I did nothing to earn it except get born into it. This"— he touched his scarlet regimental sleeve —"I earned. Until I sell out, if I sell out, I am a soldier, and damned— pardon, ladies—dashed proud of it."

Lady Atterbury cleared her throat. Before she could get in her next question, one of the other ladies asked, "Then you don't mean to abdicate? Talk is going around that you might."

"I don't know where such talk arose, except in drawing rooms such as this." He smiled to take the sting from his words, then rose to take his leave. "I never wanted to be earl, and certainly never counted on it, by Jupiter, but Preston Conover shall not stand in my father's shoes, or my brother's, while I hold breath in my body. Is that what you wanted to know, ladies?" He bowed to each in turn. "If there are no further questions, I shall wish you a good day, and thank you for an . . . entertaining tea."

The dowagers sat shamefaced, knowing even they had gone too far, and indeed, the boy handled himself well under fire. Sonia took their momentary loss of speech as an opportunity to say, "I'll just walk the major out, Your Grace."

As they walked down the hall toward where Marston stood with the major's hat and gloves, Fitz bounded up to them. His greeting of the major was enthusiastic to the point of endangering Darius's balance.

"I always seem to be apologizing for your treatment at Atterbury House," Sonia told him.

He scratched behind the dog's ears. "Think nothing of it, Miss Randolph. Fitz and I do fine."

She laughed. "I didn't mean Fitz, sir. I meant Grandmama!"

He gave her a crooked smile. "I was captured by the enemy once. Your grandmother and her friends were only slightly less humane than my French interrogators. In truth I was glad to see she keeps such a careful watch over you, the way you take up with strangers."

Sonia turned away, petting the dog. "You make me sound a veritable peagoose."

"No, no. I didn't mean that, Miss Randolph, just that you are so trusting, so good. Not everyone is worthy of your regard." He laughed, more at himself than anything. "Having said that, will you do me the honor of driving out with me this afternoon?"

"Oh, I'm sorry, Major, but I am already promised."

"I see." And he did. She had played Lady Bountiful, done her good deed for the day. Now they were even in her eyes, he supposed, and he could only thank her for her efforts on his behalf and be on his way. He accepted his hat from the butler. "I'll be off then."

Sonia could feel his hurt, despite the forced smile and the polite words. She stopped him with a touch on his arm. "Major, I really am promised for today. I would be more than pleased to have your company in the park tomorrow, though. Perhaps the children . . ."

Drat the children, he was thinking, his spirits soaring once more as he read the message in her blue, blue eyes. Then he came back to earth and remembered who, and what, he was. Yes, the children and the dog, the nanny, two footmen and a maid, anything to protect her reputation. From him. It wouldn't always be so, he promised himself, while Sonia was having to hold her hand back from smoothing the lines on his forehead.

Marston coughed and pointedly opened the door. The two sprang apart and were completing their plans for the morrow just as a carriage pulled up. When the tiger went to the horses' heads, Ansel Berke got down and strutted up the stairs when he saw Miss Randolph framed in the open doorway. He blew out his chest the better to show off his new waistcoat, green hummingbirds embroidered on crimson marcella. Then he stopped at the threshold as Darius Conover came into view. Red anger burnt up the baron's neck to his face, clashing horribly with his outfit.

Ignoring the major as if he did not exist, the baron stiffly asked if Miss Randolph was ready for their drive.

"I'll just go get my bonnet, my lord. Excuse me, Major."

Somehow, as Sonia turned to go up one side of the double arched stairwells, and Darius made to step around the other man, the baron's foot got in the way of the major's cane. Darius saved himself from falling by painfully clutching the hall table, overturning a salver of cards and invitations.

"Clumsy oaf," Berke jeered.

The officer's jaws were clenched, his hands made into fists. "Don't play your games with me, Berke. I don't like you, and you don't like me. Leave it at that."

"Or else what? Or else you'll run to Admiral Cathcart to wipe your nose? No, I won't leave it, or leave you to ruin another innocent girl. You have no business around Miss Randolph," he ranted.

In a quiet, deadly voice, Major Conover replied, "As Miss Randolph is fond of saying, she picks her own friends." The look on his face expressed what Darius thought of some of her selections.

Marston, the butler, was holding out the major's cane. He stood between the two men, pleading, "Gentlemen, gentlemen, remember where you are."

Berke took the officer's cane and broke it across his knee.

Marston bowed, turned, and with stately measure marched into the butler's pantry beside the front door. Sonia could hear the lock turn as she started down the steps.

"We'll settle this another time, I think," Darius said, nodding to Sonia.

"We'll settle it now! Name your seconds, you dastard!" Berke threw the pieces of cane across the hall.

"I don't need seconds to fight you, you little fop." Darius waved his fist under Berke's nose. "You name the time and place and I'll make you sorry you ever started this."

"You can't even fight like a gentleman!"

Darius grabbed the smaller man around the neck and practically lifted him off his feet. "Why should I? I don't see any gentlemen around." He drew one fist back.

Sonia screamed. The dog barked. The old ladies and Blanche came running.

I waited for the crash of antlers; the stags were in rut.

Chapter Thirteen

Now that was more like it! Man to man, *mano a mano*, tooth and nail. We were going to get this thing settled once and for all, the survival of the fittest, may the best man win, and all that. Of course, I knew who the best man was, bad leg notwithstanding. I'd been lifted by the major when my leg was broken, lifted as easily as I can pick up a big stick. I'd felt Ansel Berke's languid pats, and smelled the sawdust padding in his calves, even through all the scent he drenched himself in. The baron worked out occasionally to stay fit; the officer stayed fit to stay alive.

This is how it should be, combat between two males, just raw power, no weapons. The strongest wins, the loser slinks away.

Weapons in the hands of man are great equalizers: weaklings can challenge the brawniest bruiser. They are also great distancers: a man who cringes at the sight of his own blood when shaving hesitates not at all to put a bullet in someone else. Weapons make killing easy. Why, someday even females might learn how simple it is to pull a trigger!

If man had never invented swords and pistols, there would never be war, which has to be the oddest manner ever devised for thinning the population. I've heard of famine, disease, and increases of preying creatures, to weed out the old, the ill, the young, and the weak. I've never, ever heard of another system for culling out the strongest, healthiest males in their primes. Furthermore, if there were no killing weapons, human people would still be huddled by their fires, waiting for the saber-tooth tigers and cave bears to finish them off!

Ah, civilization, which makes fistfighting ungentlemanly, and killing one another the proper way to settle differences. Now I was seeing primitive man with no social veneer, lips drawn back, muscles flexed. Let the games begin.

Sonia was screaming, "Don't you dare, either one of you!" She was pulling the flowers out of the big vase in the hallway, getting ready to pour its water over the two men as if they were cats on the garden wall. The elderly ladies had run out of the drawing room and were huddled together across the hall.

"My stars!" one cried.

"My salts!" another called.

"My spectacles!" the third complained. "I can't see a bloody thing!"

Lady Atterbury picked up half of the broken cane and shook it at the two men, one of whose feet were still not touching the ground. "This is conduct unbecoming a gentleman, sirrahs! Indulging in rowdyism, and in a lady's hallway!" She didn't say which was worse. "You should be ashamed of yourselves. Now, put him down!" she demanded of the major, who did, letting go of Berke so suddenly, the baron fell to the ground, skidding on the strewn invitations. He didn't stay down, though, just kept coming at Darius on his knees. Lady Atterbury started swinging the half cane at Berke's back, and Sonia tossed her vase of water, but Fitz got in the way, ruining her aim. More water landed on the dowager than on the cursing baron. Sonia shrugged and brought the vase down on Berke's head.

Berke was out cold in a pile of porcelain, Lady Atterbury was sputtering, the dog was scampering around in the spilled flowers. The dowagers were gathered together like Macbeth's witches, cataloging every detail for future reference. Blanche was standing with her mouth open, exclaiming how no novel had ever had this much excitement—and Darius was laughing!

"Why, you—" Sonia flew at him.

Then Hugh came in.

His uniform not quite buttoned up, his hair every which way, Lieutenant Randolph rushed into the hall without a second's thought to the open door or the missing butler. He had eyes for no one but his sister, whom he immediately scooped up into his arms and spun around. "It's a boy," he shouted as loudly as he could. "A boy, Sunny! Do you know what that means?" He didn't give her time to answer, just kept spinning. "It means I can put in for transfer to the front! Papa has to let me go now that George has an heir!"

Sonia beat at his chest until he put her down. "What are you talking about, you rattlepate?" she demanded.

"George! I intercepted the messenger from Deer Park on his way to you. Didn't you hear me? Old George has a son! A month early, too, the sly devil!"

"Were you both born in a barn?" Lady Atterbury shrieked.

Hugh made a hurried bow. "Uh, good afternoon, Grandmother, Your Grace. Sorry, didn't see you in my excitement. Uh, don't suppose I should have said that, about George, I mean. My apologies, ma'am, but congratulations, Your Grace, great-great-grandson and all that." Then he tried to make a hurried departure before Lady Almeria told him what she thought of the grandchildren she already had, something she was wont to do at every occasion. "I'll just be toddling off now, visit the War Office, don't you know."

Before Hugh could make good his escape, Sonia grabbed his sleeve. "Don't you dare leave yet, Hugh! How is Jennifer?"

Hugh stared nervously at his grandmother, who'd always made him tongue-tied. "The, uh, messenger just said everyone's fine."

"What's the baby's name, you looby? Has Papa been sent for?"

"Deuce, Sunny, it's a boy. I didn't stay to hear any more." He looked over her shoulder and caught sight of three other grandes dames down the hall. He made strangling noises in his throat. Then he noticed the girl near them and brightened. "Hallo, Blanche, ladies. Uh, Lady Blanche. Meant to call on you, thank you for the dance and all, you know. Forgot, what with the news. I'm finally getting to go to fight Boney; what do you think of that? Uh, pretty dress. Call tomorrow, what?" His social obligations fulfilled to his satisfaction, Hugh turned to go, and finally began to notice a few oddities in the ancestral hall. Like a peer of the realm groaning on the floor amid potsherds and posies and the post. Hugh's eyes popped open wide. "What have you done now, Sunny? I told the governor you needed a keeper."

"Me? Why does everyone blame me?" Sonia yelled. Then she moderated her tones to a ladylike level. "I believe the two gentlemen had a difference of opinion." She waved toward the shadows where the major was leaning against the wall, having laughed himself silly all over again at the Randolph siblings' wrangling. "I daresay Major Conover can explain the details," Sonia said coldly, although the dimples were starting to show as she realized how they must all look.

Darius bowed in the recumbent nobleman's direction. "The baron took exception to my cane."

"Your cane!" Lady Atterbury snorted. "I never heard the like in all my—"

She got no further, because Hugh was striding up to Darius. "It *is* Major Conover!" He hurriedly rebuttoned his uniform coat and smoothed back his hair, then snapped a salute. "Sir, it is an honor."

"At ease, Lieutenant." Conover saluted, then leaned back against the wall. His leg was paining him like the devil after the contretemps with Berke, who was sitting up now, with the aid of a footman. The servants had finally come forward after Sonia's repeated pull on the cord. They'd been waiting for instructions from Marston; they'd have a long wait. Bigelow took charge in her usual efficient fashion: "Mop. Broom. Sticking plaster. Dry clothes. Gaol."

Hugh, meanwhile, was so in alt at meeting one of the heroes of the Peninsula that he was pacing back and forth in the hall, trampling rosebuds into the carpet. "I heard he was at the affair last night, Sunny. Couldn't believe my ears. Here I was, at the same dull ball with Major Conover! And you never let on he was coming."

Sonia was used to Hugh's passions. "If you'd been doing your duty in the ballroom, you wouldn't have missed him. And my ball was not dull."

"That's what I heard, today! Dash it, Sunny, you could have sent word to the card room!"

"But, Hugh, how was I to know you cared to meet the major?"

"How? I'm in uniform, ain't I? Everyone in the army wants to meet the major. The fellows at the barracks will be knocked cock-a-hoop that I got to see him, right here at m'grandmother's." He looked around as if wondering what in the world a top-of-the-trees officer was, in fact, doing at stodgy Atterbury House. That farrago about a cane, the prone peer, all went by the board as a new thought struck Hugh. Generally he had room for only one at a time. "Deuce take it if you couldn't put in a word with old Hokey for me, Major. They say if he don't listen to you, he don't listen to anyone."

Berke was on his feet now, looking around groggily. Sonia quickly turned to her brother. "Major Conover was on his way out, Hugh. Perhaps you can convince him what a fine fellow you are if you lend him your arm down the stairs. His cane seems a bit the worse for wear."

Like an eager puppy, Hugh offered his arm, his escort, his eternal devotion. Did the major want him to call a hackney, or should they borrow the prime rig out front, since Berke didn't look to be going anywhere soon? Maybe the major would like to come meet some of the fellows at the barracks, share a toast to Hugh's new nephew and new freedom. Was he free for dinner? Hugh knew a bang-up tavern.

Sonia looked at the awakening baron and the shambles of her grandmother's hall. Then she gazed beseechingly at the major. One look from those blue eyes and Darius allowed as how he'd like nothing better than to spend an hour or two in young Randolph's company.

"I will not have my family's dirty linen washed in public!" Lady Atterbury raged.

Sonia looked up from where she was holding a damp cloth to the back of Lord Berke's head, in the small withdrawing room. His eyes were closed, and she worried that he might be concussed. They were waiting for the doctor. The least Sonia could do, she felt, was make him comfortable, which included hushing her grandmother's angry tirade. "I am sure your friends won't say anything about George and the baby."

"George? What need have my friends got to say anything about George? Do you think the ton can't count for themselves? Half of them were at the wedding, you nimwit. What's that to the point? Half the infants born these days come early. At least George can be fairly certain he's the brat's father, which is more than I can say for a lot of treacle moon babies. No, I am talking about that disgraceful scene in my hallway, miss, the likes of which Atterbury House has never seen, I can assure you. When that gets out we'll all be laughingstocks or worse."

The baron groaned. "No one will hear a thing of it," Sonia reassured both the dowager and Lord Berke. "The servants have all been with you for years and won't be disloyal now. They know better than to gossip about the family."

"You mean they know they won't keep their jobs if they go prattling in the pubs." Lady Almeria sipped some of the sherry Sonia poured out for her.

"And I cannot believe your dearest friends would betray you by bandying the tale about."

"Oh, they'd talk, all right, if I didn't know worse dirt about their own families. Why, I could just tell Sally Jersey about Empora's daughter and the second footman. And the third footman. That would put paid to her visits to Town. I never did mention exactly why Philomena's son got sent down from Oxford, either, but she knows I could. As for Sydelle, humph! The ton always did wonder about why her last son didn't take after either side of the family."

"Grandmother!" Sonia jerked her head toward Lord Berke.

"Oh, that's all old news, and he'll be the last one to talk. Not after making such a cake out of himself." The baron held the cloth over his face and whimpered.

"Blanche will never tell either, Grandmama, she swore."

"She better not, if she knows what's good for her. After all, she just might have to take this chaw-bacon if you don't." Lady Atterbury ignored the baron's muffled protests. "No, it's that ninnyhammer of a grandson I'm worried about. His tongue runs on wheels. Loosen it a bit with Blue Ruin or whatever poison the young cockle-heads imbibe these days, and he's liable to sing his song in every officers' club and army barracks. Especially since he's gone moonstruck with hero worship."

"You don't think the, ah, major will spread the tale on his own?" Sonia asked.

Lady Atterbury hesitated a moment, then uttered a decided "No. Don't get me wrong, I don't hold the boy blameless. Too hot at hand by half. But I saw him. He left here with dignity, at least. Somehow I don't think he'll lower himself." That was as close as Lady Atterbury was going to get to approval of the disgraced earl.

Sonia nodded. She trusted him implicitly. "See, Grandmother, you have nothing to worry about then. Major Conover will keep a lid on Hugh. I'm sure he took his measure right off, and must be used to young subalterns who hang on his every word. No one will ever hear there was a fistfight in the foyer."

"You haven't thought, girl. What are we going to tell the sawbones who comes? And what about Berke's tiger, who must have seen the whole thing? To say nothing of every passerby and delivery person in Grosvenor Square. The blessed door was wide open! I'll strangle that Marston, if I ever find him."

The baron took to moaning again, so the dowager turned on him. "Stop your caterwauling, Berke. You have no one to blame but yourself. I heard enough to know who was at fault. You could have let him walk by."

Berke took the towel from his face. "You're forgetting m'sister Hermione, your own goddaughter's sister. I can't let him get away with that."

"Forget Hermione! She was no better than she should be. Why keep blaming some cad for not doing the right thing, when you should have blamed Hermione for doing the wrong thing in the first place! Besides, he said he didn't ruin her then. There is nothing to be gained now."

"Except keeping him away from other innocent young girls."

"You sapskull! He was a pariah and would have stayed that way if you hadn't stirred things up, made him look persecuted. Now he's an object of sympathy, dunderhead, and you did it yourself. If he gets taken up by the ton despite all your scandalmongering, you'll look even more the fool. You, sir, would have done better to let sleeping dogs lie."

Dogs don't lie.

Chapter Fourteen

*W*hat's in a name? Oh, I know that cat dirt about a rose by any other name, but that was Romeo and Juliet, and look what happened to them. Tippy says to remember Othello, and "He who steals my purse steals trash, something, something, but he who filches from me my good name, something, something, makes me poor indeed."

Names, good or otherwise, have little to do with truth. Ask Othello. Better yet, ask poor Desdemona. Reputations can be made, or unmade, by malicious claptrap or even circumstantial evidence. For instance, a fox with feathers in his fur is considered just as guilty as a fox with a fowl flapping in his fangs. Maybe the first fox happened upon an old pillow. And maybe the major didn't ruin Berke's sister. Try to prove either one. So how do you restore a ruined reputation?

Major Conover seems to be Miss Sonia's choice of mate, and he is equally taken with her. Even a cow could tell. Why, all they have to do is brush against each other getting into a carriage or something, and their scents are almost embarrassing. The carriage horses perk up their ears, the birds start chirping louder. Smelling of April and May, indeed. That's not what we call it.

Of course, the humans can't sniff the *eau d'amour*. (I once knew a poodle named Mon Cher. He could make sarcoptic mange sound elegant.) Men are nose-dumb. They can't tell when a fire is starting, strangers are coming, or a baby needs changing. They can't even smell rain when it's minutes away. They need us.

Anyway, since the major is so obviously Miss Sonia's pick—and I must say, having now observed the other gentlemen in the park, he is the likeliest candidate—I see no reason to delay. I have reconciled myself to the children, especially once I realized the major will want a male heir. And his smoking could be worse. He could chew the stuff like Jem in the stables, then spit it out to get on someone's feet. Lady Atterbury is not quite so antagonistic to the match, although she still suspects it to be no more than mere friendship, which will wane as Miss Sonia meets others. The only impediment I can see, beyond the major's and Miss Sonia's bound-to-be-temporary ignorance of the state of their affections, of course, is his reputation.

Social standing is very important here in London. The rats who live in the stables won't associate with the rats who live behind the dustbins. I met two of the latter, Lex and Drip, who advised me the major's case was hopeless.

"You've got *habeas corpus*," Lex pointed out. "That's the party of the first part, the dead girl, Hermione. Then your party of the second part says *nolo contendere*. He does not refute the accusation in the *modus vivendi* or accepted manner, but goes *ex patria*. The prosecution rests. The verdict is guilty."

I say, *"Amor vincit omnia,"* to which Lex replies, *"De minimis non curat lex*, the law takes no account of trifles."

Lex forages behind a solicitor's office at night.

Drip, so called because of his nose, sniffled and said, " 'E ain't never goin' t'be accepted into 'er world"— snuffle —"never dance at Almack's. Iffen 'e's any kind a gent at all, 'e'll never ask 'er to share 'is hu"— snort —"miliation. 'At's like askin' a moll rat to jump on th' trap wi' you."

Despite their discouragement, I am determined to see the major take his proper place in society, Miss Sonia by his side. She is doing all she can, going to the park with him and the children so people can see he is not an ogre. She sings his praises every chance. Even Lady Atterbury has had him back to tea, with no untoward events. Master Hugh tells everyone what a capital fellow he is, and extols his friend's acts of valor over every mug of ale. And Lady Blanche, making a foursome with the Randolphs and Conover, whispers to the other debutantes that Darius is the most romantically tragic figure she's ever known. Like a hero in one of her novels, she sighs.

It is not enough, so I have to take action. After all, what could prove a man more worthy than the affection of a dog? I positively fawn over him in the park. I dog his footsteps. I pay him the supreme compliment of trusting him with my mistress. Everyone has to see and take note: I am by his side, therefore, he is a wonderful fellow. Dogs do not lie.

"Oh dear. I am so sorry, Major, I don't know what's gotten into Fitz these days. He never used to be so . . . so coming. I'm sure the footprints will wipe off your uniform."

Sonia was even more embarrassed later that day when her dog seemed to miss the bush he was aiming at and dampened Baron Berke's shiny Hessians instead. She'd apologized profusely to the baron for braining him with the vase: "An accident, I assure you. I merely meant to toss the water to get your attention." And she tolerated the milksop's company on occasion to keep peace with her grandmother.

Berke graciously forgave her the headache and still squired her about whenever she permitted. He needed a wealthy wife more than ever. The duns were on his tail, and even his sister wasn't handing over the ready, most likely on Conare's orders. Damn Preston's black soul. Mostly, Berke just wanted Sonia Randolph because he'd be damned if he'd lose her to any loose-screw craven. Once she was his, he'd tame her madcap ways, beat them out of her if necessary, or send her off to some country place out of his way. The first thing he'd do was get rid of that unmanageable hairy beast she took everywhere with her.

"Think nothing of it, my dear," he forgave again, as a toadeater must. "Dogs will be dogs."

Sonia was careful to keep the two men apart, mainly because another confrontation could deal the major's reclamation a setback. His reacceptance into the upper ten thousand was coming along by inches instead of miles, but it was coming. If strollers did not stop to chat when Miss Randolph and the major walked along the Serpentine while the children fed the ducks, at least they nodded and smiled at the pretty picture the little girls and the black dog made. If people passed them when Sonia and Darius, Blanche and Hugh, walked along Bond Street, no one crossed to the other side or looked through him. When Darius attended the theater with Hugh and called in Lady Atterbury's box at intermission, only Rosellen Conare turned her back.

He was even receiving invitations, and not just from the military or old friends of his father's. Most of the new requests for his company came from gentlemen for an evening of whist or a day at the races, but they were tentative offers of friendship all the same. If the hosts were men with no young daughters to worry about, well, he wasn't interested in a bunch of whey-faced debs anyway. He accepted some of the invitations, preferring the company of his nieces and even the rattlepate Hugh and his young friends—when he couldn't have Sonia's company—to the heavy gambling and heavier drinking common among the leisure lords. For a man used to risking his life in battle, there was no thrill in the turn of a card.

Darius was careful not to attend any dinners or sporting events where his cousin Preston or Ansel Berke was likely to appear, not from fear of an encounter, but from fear of distressing Sonia. Part of the major's dawning acknowledgment was due to his title, part to his uniform. A good part of his acceptance, he knew, was due to Miss Randolph. Sonia was the pet of the ton within a fortnight of her come-out. She delighted the old ladies, thrilled the old men, captivated the young gentlemen, and made friends with their sisters. She listened, she laughed, she enjoyed everyone's company, even the worst bores and the most muse-struck mooncalfs. She still made time for three orphaned children. Half a dozen hostesses vied for her presence every evening; seven sprigs fought for her every dance. The least they could do was be civil to the soldier she insisted was a friend. They weren't ready to introduce Conover to their sisters or daughters, but a smile, a nod, a half bow or curtsy, couldn't harm anybody. Perhaps when he used the title . . .

No, Darius wouldn't disappoint his "friend" by creating any more scenes. And he wouldn't push

Sonia for more than friendship until he could meet her as an equal, someone she needn't be ashamed of being seen with, or who was invited to the balls and routs she attended. Even though her companionship was more than he ever dreamed of having, he knew—and he thought she knew—how much more than friendship he wanted from her. How could she not, when his heart beat like a drumroll in her presence?

The major's heart may have tattooed *Charge*, but his head was sounding *Retreat*. Don't rush her, he kept telling himself, don't try to monopolize her and ruin her chances of finding a more eligible *parti*. Don't let her be cursed for your past. So he waited and was polite when people offered him the crumbs of hospitality, for suddenly, being recognized as a member of society mattered to him. He rested, he gained back the lost weight, and he didn't harass the surgeons about declaring his left leg fit for duty. The waiting was the hardest part.

"Why does it take these stupid people so long?" Sonia fretted to Blanche one morning as they tried on bonnets at a fashionable millinery establishment. She made a face in the mirror at a cottage bonnet with artificial cherries on the brim. "Can't they see what an honorable man he is?"

"Can't *see* such a thing, Sunny," Blanche answered, not even needing to ask who the *he* was. "Handsome and broad-shouldered, assuredly, but honorable?"

"Well, he is! And kind and smart and interesting and fun. Have you ever seen him really smile, Blanche? It's like . . . like . . ." She dropped the lavender cloche.

"Like Count Minestrono's in *Araminta and the Arab Sheik*," Blanche breathed. " 'When the brooding ends and the soul's inner beauty is revealed.' "

Sonia frowned. "I don't think so."

Blanche wasn't sure if Sunny referred to the

ruched satin bonnet or the quote. "Well, they can't decide, not when his own cousin looks down on him. Conare and Rosellen have a lot of influence."

"I've seen how Rosellen looks at him, like a hungry spider looks at a fly. Then she turns away."

"Society will accept him in time, no doubt. Maybe not the highest sticklers, but opinions are swaying in his favor. If he used the title, they'd sway faster."

"He is honoring his calling and his comrades, and I respect him for that."

"So much that you'd follow the drum?" Blanche asked. "Your grandmother would have spasms for sure."

Sonia looked uncertainly at her reflection in the mirror, a hussar-style hat in her hand. "I always thought of a house in the country, with children and dogs. What about you? Should you like to travel with the army?"

"Above all things! Why, it would be like *Melissandra on the March*. Only more dusty and dirty, I expect. But think of the excitement!"

Sonia did not want to think of Major Conover or Hugh going off to war and danger. The thought wasn't exciting at all; it was frightening and upsetting. "I think Grandmama may be right. You do read too many lurid novels. Here, try this bonnet. The wide brim should set off your high cheekbones."

Blanche rushed to the mirror to see if she really did have high cheekbones. To cheer her friend, she said, "Don't worry, in a month or so everyone will have forgotten any unpleasantness in the past and he'll be invited everywhere."

"But I want to dance with him now! He is not limping half so badly. What if he goes back to Spain in a month? Besides, I am tired of going to all these silly balls and dancing with every other man in London, from empty-headed boys to empty-pocketed rakes."

"Give it time. The doors are starting to open."

Before Sonia had one measly waltz with Darius, the doors slammed shut in his face. A few even closed to Miss Randolph.

"Well, missy, you've done it now. You may as well go on back to the country and raise roses and other people's children. You'll never make a match in London, that's for certain. And I don't need any harum-scarum companion either."

"But why, Grandmama?"

"Why? Why are you the most willful chit I've ever known? Because that slowtop Elvin Randolph had the raising of you, and he never raised anything in his life right but sheep. I need my hartshorn."

"No, Your Grace, why did Lady Blanche's aunt suddenly decide I was not a good influence on Blanche?"

"It has nothing to do with influence. Philomena knew you did the girl good, got her out of those wretched novels and into prettier styles. It has everything to do with your pet. No, not that caper-witted dog, that rogue of an unacknowledged earl you've been trying to foist on the polite world. He was a wolf in wolf's clothes, and you tried to convince 'em he was a lamb. Well, you didn't pull the wool over their eyes for long, missy, and now they're mad. The tame beast's turned, and they're turning on you for bringing him into their parlors. You'll be lucky if they don't rescind your vouchers to Almack's."

"What could he have done that was so awful? I refuse to believe he compromised another girl, because he's never been anything but a perfect gentleman with me. Did he and Baron Berke have another go-round? Just what are they blaming him for this time?"

I've met a few fish in my day, but never a card-shark.

Chapter Fifteen

$\mathcal{A}$ cheat. Ivory tuner. Captain Sharp. I got that straight from one of the old carriage horses who used to take the last earl to White's. Among the privileged class, cheating at cards was a worse crime than beating one's wife. Then again, among the lower orders, stealing a loaf of bread was a worse crime than beating one's wife. There was not even a law making the latter illegal.

A male dog will half die before turning on a bitch, no matter the provocation, yet men, who spout of honor, think nothing of harming persons smaller and weaker. This is all of a piece, I suppose, with their considering women chattel. Women are not allowed to vote, hold property, take part in government, or manage their own estates, because they are not deemed competent. Yet, and here is the part that truly muddles my mind, men let women raise their children!

Anyway, from what I could hear from gossip on the street, the pigeons who roost at Boodles' at night, Major Conover has been accused of cheating at cards by—who else?—Ansel Berke. Lord Conare was in the game, held in a private room of Scully's, a gambling hell in Half-Moon Street. Conare, predictably, seconded the charge of double dealing. Two other noblemen held hands in the fateful game, but they were so castaway, they could only recall seeing Conover enter the room. They were assured by both Conare and Berke that Conover had, indeed, won their blunt. They were suitably outraged to be shown the extra ace, found on the next deal, after Conover was gone.

The major had gone to Scully's with Captain McKinnon of the Home Guard, the pigeons understood, but they separated after half an hour or so. McKinnon lost sight of Conover in the smoke and crowded rooms, he later said. The major took a few turns at hazard, played a couple of rounds of vingt-et-un, and held the faro bank for a short while. Then he wandered into some of the back parlors, according to Scully himself, looking for more interesting play. After that he went home to bed—and awoke to find himself branded a cheat.

I smelled Preston Conover's hand in the plot: another vicious whispering campaign, with Berke doing the dirty work, more charges that couldn't be disproved, Major Conover an outcast again. I could howl at the injustice of it. All my hard work! By St. Bernard's beard, if I had that mangy Conare here, I'd tear him limb from limb, I'd shred him from guts to gizzard, I'd . . . be chained in the backyard.

If a man fuzzes the cards, loads the dice, or deals from the bottom, he mightn't pay his debts either. No one will play with him. They won't even talk to him. Men don't seem to mind losing fortunes honestly; they only care when they think they've been diddled.

Strange, no other creature but man gambles. Tippy says betting can be a disease, just like distemper and rabies. Sometimes men who cannot afford to lose gamble just as hard as those who can. They only need a stake and a little luck. Or just a marked deck.

"You can't send a letter, Sunny, it ain't proper." Hugh was having breakfast at Atterbury House at his sister's insistence, and not enjoying his gammon and eggs at all. A man didn't like a bear garden jaw with his kippers. At least Lady Atterbury never left her chambers till noon.

"I didn't send a letter, Hugh," Sonia insisted. "I sent Fitz." She was too distracted to sit still, which wasn't doing much for Hugh's digestion either.

"And?"

"And nothing! A footman brought Fitz home. He said there was no message, nothing. The young misses have already been sent to visit their mother's people in Lyme. That's all the footman knows, or would say." She banged her cup down on the table. "I've got to see him, Hugh!"

Hugh spread jam on a piece of toast and pondered the matter. "Can't see how you can if he don't want you to. He's got the right of it, too. Got to keep your name out of the bibble-babble. Best you stay out of the coil."

Sonia snatched the toast out of her brother's hand. "Hugh, you don't mean to say you think he's guilty?" she demanded before taking a bite of the bread.

"I never said I do, just that you should keep clear while he's under such a cloud."

"Then you do believe Darius would never, ever do something dishonorable?"

"Darius, eh? I thought the wind sat in that quarter. Too bad, sis, you'll have to set your cap at some other poor sod. The governor will never hear of you marrying a dirty dish." He held a hand up in de-

134

fense. "Not that I think he ain't honorable. Play cards with him m'self any time, if my pockets weren't always to let." He made sure she was eating while he buttered another slice. "And look who's laying evidence against him. Everyone knows Conare wants the title and Berke wants you."

"Me?" she squeaked, spitting out crumbs. "You mean this is all my fault?"

"Don't be a ninny. The feud with Berke goes back years before you put your hair up and your skirts down. Be hard to prove they set the whole thing up, though, with the only witnesses admitting they were drunk as wheelbarrows. It'd be Berke's word against Conover's, if Berke said it outright. Instead it's all lies and rumors."

"Then what's to be done?" Sonia wanted to know.

Hugh swallowed a large bite. "I told him to ship out. Nobody'd think the worst of him, least of all the fellows who've fought by his side for years. He said he's thinking on it."

She pounded her fist on the table. "It would be just like him to think he could simply go off without saying good-bye. Well, he can't."

Hugh munched some more. "Yes, he can. Better that way. Can't say I want m'sister in such a hugger-mugger mess."

"Hugh." He knew that tone from old. He left his toast and bolted for the door. "Hugh Randolph, you get that muttonhead of a major in Grosvenor Square Park at two o'clock this afternoon or else."

"Or else what?" he asked from the door, sure he didn't want to know, wishing his orders had come through yesterday.

"Or else I'll go to Ware House myself, or I'll inform Grandmama he compromised me, or I'll just tell Blanche Carstairs you wet your bed till you were twelve."

Sonia sat on the same bench where she'd first spoken to Darius just a few weeks ago. It seemed like forever, he was so much in her thoughts. Now he could be leaving England, and she might never see him again. She wouldn't think of that. Instead she'd let her anger cover the pain, anger that he'd go away without a farewell, without leaving her one last memory to cherish. She sat rigid on her bench, her hands folded in her lap, a statue in a blue velvet pelisse. Even Fitz couldn't tease her into playing.

Maisie sat on the neighboring bench with her knitting, and Ian was getting up a flirtation with two nannies pushing prams. A nearby clock struck the hour. He was late. He wasn't coming.

Then he was there, looking more handsome than she'd ever seen him, now that his face was fuller and not so wearied. He bowed to her, but didn't take her hand or sit next to her. He didn't speak, either.

She cleared her throat. "You came."

"Hugh seemed to think it was worth my life, and his, had I not."

"But you did not want to." It was a statement, not a question. If he heard the hurt in her voice, he did not, could not, respond. He stared toward the trees, not looking at her.

"No, it is not wise. And there is nothing to say."

Nothing to say? Sonia bit her lip. "I, ah, wanted to know about the children. Will they be happy in Lyme?"

"Happier than here, I hope. Suzannah's parents are well on in years, but they love the girls. They used to visit, before . . . Her old nurse is still there, anxious to help coddle them, I am sure, so they'll do. They wanted to say good-bye, you know, but it was very early in the morning."

"I see," she said, but her coldness told him that she didn't see at all, didn't understand that he couldn't have borne another emotional scene. 'Twas hard enough parting with the three moppets he'd come to love as his own, without watching them cling one last time to her. Not when he had hoped for so much more.

"They swore they would write. And they were excited about visiting their grandparents and the seashore. I promised they could each have a pet of their choice when they got there. Benice can pick between a puppy and a kitten, and Gen already decided she wants a pony. Tina seems content with her stuffed Mimi. Not quite fair to the grandparents, I'll admit, but now they have something to think about on the journey."

"That was clever of you." She pleated the velvet of her pelisse. "They are wonderful children. I'll miss them."

"I, ah, had my solicitor draw up new papers, naming their grandfather as guardian if . . . just if. Milo wanted them to be raised at Ware, but this is better, I think. I know I have no right to ask you to look after them or anything—you'll have children of your own before long—but could you write to them? About Fitz or whatever, just at first, so they don't feel abandoned?"

She waved that aside. Naturally she would write the children, and visit them, too, but what about her? Didn't he care that she'd feel lost, abandoned? "Shall you write?" she asked, knowing how improper, how forward, was her question.

Darius chose to misinterpret. "The children? Of course, if I can."

Sonia thought that if she had a gun, she'd shoot him right then and save the French the trouble. "When do you sail?"

"Sail?" Now he turned to look at her, but Sonia had her head down so the brim of her bonnet hid her face. "I thought you knew, I am not rejoining the regiment just yet."

She looked up at that, blue eyes filled with hope. "But Hugh said . . ."

He turned away quickly. "I thought about it, but I cannot." He started to pace along the path in front of her, jabbing his cane into the loose dirt. "I made a mistake years ago." He paused at her sharp intake of breath. "No, not with the girl. I had nothing to do with Hermione but a few dances here and there. The mistake was in not meeting Berke. Milo thought it best, since her family already suffered so much grief, and I was off to the war anyway. He said he'd rather chance losing me to a better cause than a sordid affair."

"He loved you," she said softly.

"I shouldn't have listened. The hatred festered in Berke, and backing down did me no good. I let him win without firing a shot. Berke and the other highborn asses who rule this town control my life. I cannot go where I choose, I cannot make friends where I wish. I cannot speak my mind. Or my heart."

That traitorous organ made him turn back to Sonia, to see if she understood what he could not put into words, what his circumstances and his principles would not permit him to say.

Sonia nodded. At least his suffering matched her own. She hadn't been mistaken, then. The last threads of her anger melted away.

He went on: "I am sorry for so many things. I regret my troubles have rubbed off on you, but I am not sorry to have had your . . . friendship. Never that."

"You intend to duel him, don't you?"

"It's the only way. The first time they called me lily-livered for not meeting him. I didn't care. I knew I was no coward, and Milo knew, and the men who served with me and under me knew. They were all who mattered. I did not have to prove anything to these useless, empty-lived parasites. Now I do, so I can reclaim my birthright, my freedom. I need to live my life the way *I* want."

"What if you kill him?" She couldn't bear to think of the other.

One side of his mouth lifted in a grim half smile. "Thank you for the confidence. I'll have to leave the country, of course. The family has property in the Colonies if the general won't take me back. But I'll try not to have it come to that if I can."

"Please," she told him, bringing the rest of the smile to his face. Then she asked "When?"

"You don't need to know that. You know too much already. Lud, a proper gentleman never discusses such things with a lady."

"When?" she asked again, quietly.

"Hugh was right, you are a determined little minx. No matter, for I do not know the time or place yet, and would never reveal them if I did. You might get some odd notion in that thick, pretty head of yours to interfere or notify the magistrates. No, don't look so innocent. I can almost hear the wheels spinning in your brainbox. I haven't confronted Berke yet, although I doubt he'll be hard to find. He's waiting for my challenge so he can have the choice of weapons. He knows I'd pick swords, for I am much the better fencer, even with a bad leg. With swords there is less chance of an unintentional mortal wound, too. That's not what he wants, so he'll make himself available. This afternoon in the park, tonight at some gaming hell or other."

"And there is no other way?" Sonia held her hand out, and he took it in his.

"Believe me, this is not the way I would have chosen. Berke thrust it upon me, and now it is the only solution."

She nodded. "I do understand."

He squeezed her hand in his larger one and tried to make light of the matter. "What, no arguments? No stiff lip and crossed arms? No stamping feet as Miss Randolph demands her own way?"

She shook her head.

"What? Not even one plea or threat to make me change my mind?" he teased. "Don't you care?"

The tears shining in her eyes told him how much

she cared, but her words only said: "How can I come between a man and his honor?"

Easily. You hit him behind the knees.

Chapter Sixteen

$\mathcal{N}$ow he couldn't stand on his honor, or on his leg.

I looked up at the trees, searching for the squirrel I was supposed to be chasing. What do you know, the little nutter got away! As I rushed past, though, I heard an audible snap as the major's bad leg gave way beneath him. Once the chaos died down, the sawbones eventually found a bit of shrapnel in the leg when he went to set it. He said that's why the thing never healed in the first place. Now the major will not even have a limp, once the bone mends. Oh, what a good dog I am!

So was I wrong, or does the end justify the means? Darius seems to feel that a life without honor is not worth living. I, however, need him alive for what I consider the greater goal. I never argue with another's beliefs. He had his, I had mine. Mine won.

Still, this honor thing bothers me like a flea bite I can't quite reach. Tippy says to remem-

141

ber the "But Brutus is an honorable man" bit. Sure, with his knife in his best friend's back.

Keeping the promises that suit one, repaying gaming debts and not merchants' bills, this is not honor. Honor is when no creature molests another at the water hole.

Tippy says that what goes around comes around, yet I am satisfied with the results of my actions. There will be no challenge while the major is flat on his back. There will be no duel while he cannot leave his house.

Happily, and the more so for being unforeseen, he also gave up his cigarillos. The stench in his bedroom was too great even for the major, when he couldn't step outside or stand by the window to make the noxious smoke dissipate. Unfortunately, he took up drinking. What goes around comes around?

Master Hugh moved into Ware House to help the major and his batman, Robb. Then some of Hugh's friends came to call, to help bear the major company. Without the children, the place soon resembled a barracks, with hard drinking and gambling. The other officers made a point of playing cards with Major Conover, standing by one of their own, as it were, and drinking toasts to his health.

I took to visiting Ware House evenings when Miss Sonia was out on her social rounds. This was better than sitting up on the carriage box with the driver, who tipped his jug a few times himself. At least at Ware House there was food. The major held no grudges, so most nights I was also offered a sip of something, which I refused after watching his friends muddle their minds, curdle their stomachs till they cast up accounts, turn mean, sleepy, sad, or just plain silly. The next day they drank the hair of the dog! The hair of the dog! That's disgusting!

They say Dionysius gave wine to men as a

blessing. Some favor he did them! The god taught Icarius how to ferment his grapes, the story goes, and the villagers killed the first vintner in a drunken rage, thinking he'd poisoned them! They hid his body under a tree, and Icarius's family would be looking for him still if his dog hadn't stayed howling at the grave. Good dog, Moera. They named a star after her, too.

Robb makes sure the worst drunks get sent home, and the belligerent ones are not invited back. The batman and Hugh—on Miss Sonia's orders—and I, for obvious reasons, keep watch over the major like three hens with one chick. We don't let the visitors tire him, we won't let him use the crutches until the physician gives approval. He is healing; he hasn't got Berke's bullet in him; he is not on some boat for America. I am delighted. I just hope Major Conover isn't drinking to drown his sorrows.

Sonia was still a Toast. Everyone knew a duel had been avoided by her dog's clumsiness, which they thought hilàrious. Anytime a nobleman falls on his arse, especially one who disdains the title, society is amused. They all wanted to hear Miss Randolph's account. As soon as Hugh revealed that the major had indeed intended to call Ansel Berke out, that a challenge would be forthcoming directly he was fit, the ton gave Darius back some respect. They might laugh at him, but they did not despise him so much. Curiously, the charge of cowardice had been more a black mark against him than the trumped-up accusations of cheating. Hugh was relieved, and so was Admiral Cathcart, who made the trip from three doors away to visit the fallen officer. And laugh.

Lady Atterbury swore she never wanted to see the mongrel again, that he'd brought nothing but trouble. Elvin Randolph should be horsewhipped, she decreed, for foisting a hobbledehoy female and her harum-scarum hound on unsuspecting gentle-people. Then she commandeered all of Blanche's novels, shut herself in her bedchamber, and didn't come out for days.

She gave copious orders through Bigelow that under no circumstances was Sonia to visit the household across the square, no, not even if her own brother was there. Sonia was not permitted to stay home, either. Nor, under the direst of threats, was she to create any more scandals. Bigelow's translation: "Bachelor fare. Ape-leader. Great-Aunt Sophrina in Yorkshire." Sonia didn't even know she had a Great-Aunt Sophrina in Yorkshire.

Lady Atterbury, or Bigelow, also had a few choice words for the disappearing butler: "Guard the front door, or leave by the back door." Every time Miss Randolph or her dog went by, Marston wished he were tied to the hall table, like Jason to the mast, to resist the temptation to flee. But he stayed and held the door, accepted calling cards and nosegays, and sighed with relief when Miss went out of an evening. He nearly wept with thanksgiving when she came home without incident.

So Sonia resumed the social whirl. If she was considered too ramshackle by the highest sticklers, keeping low company and getting into scrapes, she behaved prettily enough for the rest of the Quality. If she had to go out, she decided, she would show the shallow elite what a Randolph was made of, not hide her head nor wear the willow. She wore her prettiest gowns, gathering compliments and admirers like fallen leaves. She laughed with them over Warebourne's predicament, when she was not staunchly defending him. Mr. Brummell was heard to chuckle at Fitz's antics, and Sir Montescue Pimford wrote a poem to Miss Randolph's loyalty to her friends.

Hugh raved to the major about Sunny's success, and the other officers reported that Miss Randolph danced like a dream and smiled like an angel. Darius had another drink.

Unfortunately, Sonia's foray into society threw her into close association with Lady Rosellen Conare and her brother, Ansel Berke. Sonia could not renege on previous commitments without seeming horribly rude, so she learned to tolerate the baron's company. Perhaps she could make him see what a goosish thing this was, his pursuit of vengeance. She even felt sorry for him. Pursuing heiresses was degrading enough.

"I'm glad to see you laughing at the bounder," Berke gloated. "For a moment there I was worried. I know how you females admire a uniform. And your tender sensibilities must have been aroused by the unfortunate orphans. Very proper sentiments, my dear. No one can fault you for having a gentle heart. Now, of course, you've discovered for yourself what a paltry fellow he is. I'm glad. Now I can reveal that as soon as this unpleasantness is over, I plan to ask you a particular question," he said with a simpering smile, while his teeth gnashed at the delay. His creditors were lining up at his door. He needed some crumb to toss them. "Dare I hope what your answer will be?"

He could hope all he wanted. She didn't feel that sorry for him.

Darius thought he'd be ready for Bedlam if he didn't get out of the house soon. For sure they'd have no china left, the way he bounced it off the walls. And if he had to listen to more praise for Miss Randolph from men who could call on her, go riding with her, dance with her, hold her, blast them, he would soon be calling out half the British nobility and all of the Home Guard!

So he exercised his leg while his watchdogs were still abed, and the confounded real dog was scrounging breakfast at his own house across the square. He couldn't chance Fitz getting under his feet and toppling him again. He refused any other setbacks. The leg healed remarkably quickly this time without the piece of shot. Darius was strong and healthy now, never having taken a fever or an infection from this recent surgery. Recuperation was swift, surprising even the medicos from the War Office. He was not fit to sit a horse yet, so there was no talk of his rejoining his unit, but he was fit enough to go out and kill someone, though no one spoke of the duel. It was illegal, after all.

Having satisfied the doctors of his health, Darius moved downstairs, where he could get to the rear courtyard to gain strength and proficiency with the crutches. He refused to try the park, where someone—someone with blond hair and blue eyes, for instance—might see him stagger about. Watching from the front windows as she exercised the dog in the square early in the mornings did even more to speed his recovery. Finally he was able to join her.

The crutches were just about the only thing holding Darius back from taking Sonia in his embrace; holding the exuberant dog's collar so he didn't jump was just about all that was keeping Sonia from throwing her arms around the major. Then they remembered where they were and that nothing had been said between them.

"How nice to see you out and about, Major Conover, and looking so well."

"And you are looking lovelier than ever, Miss Randolph. Thank you for the basket of fruit and the other treats from your kitchens."

So it went. They compared letters from the children, the progress of her brother's promotion, the health of Lady Atterbury and Blanche. Small talk, but they were together. They spoke more with their eyes, the briefest of touches when they both petted the dog at once. He came every morning after that and took over Fitz's exercise, to rebuild his own muscles, he said. He threw sticks, played keep-away, and hobbled around and around the square until he graduated from crutches to a cane. Every morning he purchased a posy from the flower girl to tuck in Sonia's bonnet or pin to her gown. Every morning they all shared meat pasties from the pieman, who was growing wealthy on the little entourage. Sonia was still escorted by her maid and footman, and Conover's batman, Robb, came along, too, at first to make sure his master didn't overdo, then to enjoy the company. Maisie Holbrook often went home with a posy in *her* mobcap, too. And Fitz invariably wolfed his pie down so fast, then looked so piteously hungry, that the major usually bought him another. Then they all went to sit with the admiral for a bit, Darius content just to watch Sonia as she told the old gentleman about this party or that play.

Darius never knew such peace. He tried to convince himself that this was enough, if he never had more. He didn't believe himself for a minute.

Sonia felt she merely existed for most of her day and night. She really came alive only for the two hours in the morning. "Do you think you might be up to a picnic?" she asked hesitantly, fearful he might refuse.

He knew he should. Nothing was changed; she should not be with him.

"I went on a lovely picnic to Richmond last week. The gardens were beautiful."

He knew all about it, having heard from one officer how exquisite she looked in a teal blue hussar-style riding habit. "You know, the kind with braid and trim up and down." The fellow used his hands to show where the trim went. He was lucky he could still use a fork. Darius was treated by another gentleman to an account of how Miss Randolph sat her roan mare as if she were born there, which she nearly was, according to Hugh: "M'mother was a notable horsewoman. The only thing she and the governor had in common, besides us, of course."

Darius could almost picture Sonia on horseback, wind tousling her golden curls and bringing a flush to her cheeks. Then again, he could picture other ways for her hair to be tousled and her cheeks to be flushed. No, he really should not be around her. Not if he hoped to maintain any sanity whatsoever.

"The physicians have forbidden me to ride yet," he said with both relief and regret.

"Then we could take the carriage," she hurried on. "And we don't have to go as far as Richmond, so your leg won't be jostled. We could just take the coach to a grassy place off the carriage path in Hyde Park."

He was tempted. Oh, how he was tempted. Sonia on a blanket in the sun, away from prying eyes and wagging tongues . . .

"And we'll invite Hugh and Blanche to come along for propriety's sake," she pressed, determined to have more time with him, one way or another.

Thud, thud, tap. That was two legs and a cane coming back to earth. "And I suppose the dog, too? Very well, as long as he doesn't dunk me in the Serpentine."

The day set for the picnic was not ideal. Hugh thought it might shower. Blanche thought it might be buggy. Robb thought the ground might be too damp for the major to sit on. Sonia and Darius were going, period.

They took two carriages. To Hugh's delight, he got to drive the major's curricle, with the highbred bays. Blanche sat with Hugh, and Robb stood at the back as tiger and guardian of the beloved matched pair. Sonia and Darius followed in the dowager's open landaulet, with Maisie and Fitz and the picnic basket. Ian rode with the driver.

Because the ton didn't parade at such an unfashionable hour, they had the park nearly to themselves. Nursemaids and governesses found the day too dismal to linger with their charges. Sonia didn't notice the overcast skies, and Darius was pleased the gabble-grinders would not have Sonia's name to chew. Hugh found a spot where the tanbark dipped close to the river, and a little knoll and some trees made a pretty vista. They took a short walk while the servants tethered the horses and spread blankets and pillows and enough food to feed twice their number. Or half their number and Fitz.

They passed one other couple, Sir Wesley Norbert and Mrs. Quentin-Jones, who were less likely to run to the tattle-baskets than most, so Darius was able to relax. He was grateful, in fact, to sink down onto the blankets with his back propped against a tree and a cushion under his leg, after their brief stroll. He wasn't used to carriage rides or uneven ground. Besides, sitting down, he didn't have to concentrate on where he was putting his feet. He could stare at Sonia to his heart's content, drinking in the sight of her in nile green jaconet, with clusters of yellow rosebuds and ribbons strewn around. Who cared if the sun did not shine? She was springtime to him.

The servants had a blanket and basket of their own, so Sonia got to fuss over Darius, heaping his plate, filling his glass, asking at least once a minute if he was comfortable. "You don't have to try so hard, sweet Sonia," he whispered. "I am content just being with you." Neither Blanche nor Hugh commented on Sonia's blushes or shy, answering smile. Blanche was discovering that Hugh's war stories were even more exciting than her romance novels, and he was feeling less a Sunday soldier with a nice young girl hanging on his every word. Sonia and Darius could have been in another world for all they cared.

The food was gone too soon, and the ground *was* beginning to feel damp through the blankets, yet no one wanted to go home. There was still a bit of wine left and some lemonade, so they gave themselves another few moments.

Then a group of horsemen rode along on the path. Instead of passing by, they dismounted and tied their horses to bushes and branches, before approaching the little group under the tree. There were five of them, one with a cherry-striped waistcoat, one with canary trousers, and one with a satisfied smirk on his face. Ansel Berke.

Cry "Havoc!" and let slip the dogs of war.

Chapter Seventeen

$\mathcal{T}$rust the bloodthirsty Romans to come up with a cheery turn of phrase like that. They really did have dogs of war, you know, whole packs of huge canines that they let loose before their invading armies, to soften up the enemy lines, as it were.

Do you know how they got those dogs to fight like that? They starved them! That's right. They did throw them the occasional arm or leg, to teach them that people were food.

I can see an army of bees. Geese maybe, but dogs? If they were not starving or protecting someone they love, they'd be stopping off at every bush. And I'm sorry to say this, but we have been known to fight over the same bone. Then again, one bitch in heat and your whole battalion goes to the dogs!

Why would dogs go to war anyway? Do you think the *perros* of Spain care whether it's the French or the British who overrun their country, decimating the fields and forests? Between them they take every *pollo* and rabbit, leaving *nada* for man or *mousito*. Peon and pup will starve either way. *Madre de gatos*, war is hell on the hounds, too!

Then again, some wars are inevitable.

"We have some unfinished business, Conover," Berke announced when he was a few yards away. Hugh and the girls scrambled to their feet, and the servants hurried over, forming a protective ring around the blanket. Darius stayed where he was, reclining against the tree trunk.

"Not in front of the ladies, I think" was his only reply.

"He's right," one of the baron's companions said. Sonia recognized him as one of Rosellen's foppish court. "Not good ton, old man. Mustn't sully delicate ears and all that."

Berke scowled at the pomaded dandy. He'd only brought the pack of useless caper-merchants along because he did not want to confront Warebourne alone. The skirter was too eager to use his fists. And Berke had to get this settled soon. Conare had paid his most pressing debts, on the condition that Berke bring matters to a head. As soon as he'd received word from Sir Norbert that Warebourne was in the park, Berke knew he had to act today. Besides, he thought his bravado would make him look nobler in Miss Randolph's eyes. Or Lady Blanche's, if it came to that.

He bowed to Sonia, then to Blanche. He threw his chest out, in a new plum satin waistcoat printed with pink cabbage roses, and announced, "My apologies, ladies, but I dare not let the dastard get away." He turned back to his hand-picked audience. "I'm afraid he'll find another reason to cry off. First he hid behind his brother, then his uniform. Next he found a dog to make his excuses." He paused while the men around him laughed. "Now he hides behind a woman's skirts."

Darius was still comfortably propped against the

tree, an insultingly casual reaction to Berke's cock-of-the-walk swagger. "I don't consider a picnic in Hyde Park in broad daylight to be precisely hiding, Baron. I just find you de trop at this moment."

Berke started to get red in the face. "I don't care what you think, you makebait. I've been waiting and waiting for you to stick your nose outside. If you can stand, you can duel."

"He can't," Sonia put in before Darius could answer. "We came in the carriages"— she waved to show how close they were parked —"and all the servants helped."

Darius frowned. "Hugh, take the ladies away."

"Dash it, Major, you said I could be your second. How can I make the arrangements if I'm off nurse-maiding two chits?"

"That was not a request, Lieutenant," Darius stated in a voice used to being obeyed, and instantly.

"Don't you dare pull rank on my brother at a picnic, Darius Conover, because you cannot order me around anyway. I am not leaving." Sonia was in her usual try-to-stop-me mode: arms crossed, feet firmly planted, a look of determination in her blue eyes that could have stopped Boney in his tracks.

Darius shook his head. Someone really had to take that chit in hand one of these days. He smiled, thinking about being the one. Then he turned to the dog, who was wagging his tail next to him. He put one hand on Fitz's back to pull himself up. "It's the least you can do, old son. Now sit, sir." He reached down for his cane. "And stay. There has been enough interference from you willful Randolphs. The dog should obey me, at least." He took two steps nearer Berke. "As you can see, I can walk."

"Aha! What did I tell you?" Berke crowed to his cronies. "The pudding-heart was just stalling!"

"Sonia, sweetheart," Darius said, looking right

at Berke, "pour me a glass of wine, will you, my dear?"

Hugh's mouth fell open, and one of the men behind Berke snickered. "Dutch courage, eh?"

Sonia bit her lip to keep from laughing, but Berke worked himself into a rage at the endearments, as Darius knew he would.

"Why, you miserable mawworm, to be insulting a gently bred female with familiarity like that! Dueling is too good for you. You ought to be horsewhipped!"

Sonia, meanwhile, poured the last of the wine into a glass and handed it to Darius. "Here, darling." She smiled and batted her lashes at him.

The major's lips twitched as he took the glass and went another few steps closer to Berke. When only a foot or two separated them, he told the baron, "Very few things in this world will give me as much satisfaction as putting a bullet through you. Perhaps this is one of them." With which he tossed the contents of his glass in Berke's face. He watched as the red wine dripped down the baron's chin and onto his starched cravat. "There, now your neckcloth matches your waistcoat. Perhaps you'll start a new fashion." He turned his back on the peer and carefully wiped his fingers on a napkin Sonia thoughtfully provided. "Thank you, my dear. Oh yes," he tossed back over his shoulder. "Consider yourself challenged. If you'll be so good as to name your seconds, I'm sure my enthusiastic young friend here shall be delighted to call."

"No!" Berke raged. "We'll settle the details now in case you decide to run off to the army again. Let everyone see the thing was done right. You challenged, so I get the choice of weapons."

One of the Tulips lisped, "But you mustn't pick swords, Baron. Not when the fellow's practically a cripple. Noblesse oblige and all that."

Au contraire, mes amis." Darius twisted the top of his cane. The sheath fell away and he suddenly held a long, thin rapier in his hand. Before Berke's horrified eyes, the blade swished through the air, whistled past his ear, and sliced off, not one, but two of the buttons on his waistcoat. "Go ahead. Choose swords."

"Pistols," Berke croaked. "Pistols."

"Excellent. Shall we say two days hence? That should give you enough time to find a surgeon, for do not fool yourself into believing I mean to delope. Unless, of course, you wish to retract your statements concerning a certain card game now, in front of these witnesses."

"Never!"

Darius held the sword to Berke's neck. "I do not believe we need to trouble the ladies further with the time and place, do you?"

"No, no. As long as it's settled."

"It's settled, all right. I wouldn't miss it for the world."

The drizzle started when the subdued group was packing the baskets and blankets. Darius insisted Blanche and Maisie ride with Sonia in the landaulet, its cover drawn, while he rode in the open curricle with Hugh.

"Don't argue, for once," the major told Sonia when she protested. "Hugh and I have things to discuss. This will save time. And I have been out in far worse. I am not like to expire from an inflammation of the lungs in the next two days."

Sonia was not amused. She climbed stiffly into the carriage and did not speak to Blanche or her maid on the ride home. She did clutch the damp dog to her side, oblivious to the damage to her gown.

Blanche's aunt's residence was closest, so they dropped her off first. A sober-faced Hugh got down to walk Blanche to her door, after she hugged Sonia good-bye.

Ian handed Miss Randolph out at Atterbury House. Marston started down the steps with a large black umbrella, until he saw the glum expressions on all the faces. He marched back up, umbrella and all. Bad enough he had to face disgrace in the hallway; he didn't have to go outside looking for it.

Darius climbed down from the curricle and caught up with Sonia under the portico's shelter. He was breathing hard from the exertion, and he looked back to see Hugh hunched over at the ribbons, sitting in the rain waiting for him. Robb was at the horses' heads, stroking them. "Damn and blast!" Darius muttered. "This isn't the way—"

Sonia put her hand on his sleeve. "I know, you mustn't keep the horses standing."

"I shan't be in the park tomorrow morning, you know. There are too many things needing to be done."

Sonia thought of how he must hire carriages and book passages, in case he had to flee. He needed to see his solicitor and his man of business and his bank. She nodded.

"It's better this way," he said, putting his hand over hers, then bringing her hand to his lips.

"Better for whom?"

"Just better. I hate good-byes. And we had today, didn't we?"

"Yes, it was lovely." She tried to smile for him.

"There's my brave girl," he said, still holding her hand. "I'd tell you not to worry, but—"

"But that would be foolish, like telling me not to breathe. I'll pray for you."

"I know you will. And trust me, Sunny." He brushed a damp curl back under her bonnet. "I—no, just trust me."

"I do. Now go before Hugh takes a chill and misses his big chance, and before you see I am not so brave at all."

"No good-byes?"

She shook her head. "No good-byes, just Godspeed."

He kissed her hand again and then bent toward

her and quickly brushed his lips over hers. He turned and started down the stairs.

"Darius, wait!" Sonia ripped one of the sodden yellow rosebuds off her gown and tossed it to him. Darius caught the bit of silk in his hand, carefully placed it inside his coat, next to his heart, and bowed. Then he left without looking back.

Everyone in London knew of the duel. Berke made sure of that, especially since the location remained a secret so the authorities couldn't interfere. Lady Atterbury closed the house to callers. If anyone was laying this pottage in her dish, she didn't want to know about it. Uneasily she felt she might have done something to avoid the imbroglio, spoken to Rosellen or sent Sonia out of town. Deuce take it, she was just a tired old lady. She decided to have palpitations instead of pangs of remorse.

Marston was grateful. With no visitors, he didn't have to dart into the butler's pantry for a nip. He kept a flask of the old duke's port right in his tailcoat.

Bigelow declared the whole household was going to hell in a handcart, then out of boredom she picked up one of the discarded novels. "Trash," she declared. "Moral turpitude." Then, "Oh my."

So there was no one to insist Sonia keep her appointments, or keep her head up despite the gossip making the rounds. Which was a good thing, since Miss Randolph just stayed in her rooms. She didn't read, wouldn't see Blanche or Hugh, never opened her father's latest letter. She did not eat much, and she even sent Fitz out with Ian for the dog's exercise. Strange, Ian commented to Maisie, the dog's coat was usually damper before his walk than after.

Swans mate for life.

Chapter Eighteen

More men than women remarry after the death of their spouse. Men are more conscious of a need for an heir; they are also more helpless. The men are used to having someone pamper them, or miss having a person around who cannot quit if she dislikes the position.

Women, conversely, remarry less, especially if they find themselves well off, like Lady Atterbury and her friends. For the first time in their lives they have a modicum of freedom and independence, with no father or husband as overlord. They have friends, entertainments, the willing paramour or two. For some women, one taste of married life is enough to convince them they do not need second helpings.

Of course, there are some women who wear black for the rest of their lives out of fondness for their departed husbands. Some of them just hang the crepe in their heart and never find another man they could love so well.

Miss Sonia is loyal. She never forgets her old friends; she never kept another "pet." Her mare, Dilly, does not count; that's transportation. She writes to her father every week, never speaks ill of George's wife, Jennifer, does not buy French lace. She is true-blue. I taught her well.

It took Miss Sonia eighteen years to settle on Darius Conover. I did not have another eighteen years to wait for her to find another mate. Her heart broken, she might go back to Berkshire to mourn. I'd already tried my luck there at finding her a father for her children. Worst of all, by King Arthur's Clavall, she might decide never to marry!

Besides, I like the major.

So it looks like I'm going to have to play *Canis ex machina* again. I'm ready, I just cannot see my way clear.

I cannot use the same technique as last time. The major is too downy a cove to fall for the same trick twice. And his legs are much stronger. I could knock the baron down, but there is no guarantee he'd break his leg, and they'd just go at it later. These two are determined to commit mayhem on each other.

I am preparing myself to make the ultimate sacrifice. I'll leap between the major and the bullet if I have to. My father would face a horde of wolves to protect his lambs, if there were still wolves in England. My mother would fight to the death any threat to her pups. I could do no less. I was ready.

The gathering of gentlemen, mostly officers, at Ware House lasted well past midnight, with songs and laughter and fine wines and food. In the usual way of soldiers before battle, everything was spoken of except the duel. Conover's friends left with hearty backslaps and calls of "See you tomorrow," or "Remember that mill on Saturday next."

After they left, Darius sent Hugh up to bed and

told Robb to get some sleep, too. He opened the door for Fitz to go across the square, but the cork-brained mutt stayed sprawled by the fire. "Stay, then. I'll send you home later."

Darius went back to his study for a final check that everything had been taken care of. When he threw another log on the fire, the dog followed him, collapsing in front of the hearth with a sigh, as though the effort were too much. The major smiled and turned to his desk and the lists he'd spent two days making. Things had been so much easier when he only had to face death at the hands of the French. He had no property then, no dependents. Robb would see to his horse and personal possessions; Milo would look after everything else.

Thinking of Milo, Darius touched the letters left on his desk, one for each of his brother's daughters. He drew the family signet ring off his finger and placed it on the letter for Benice, the eldest. Then he tenderly took Milo's watch out of his own pocket and centered it atop Gen's letter. On little Tina's he put one of his own treasures, which he carried with him on all the marches and transports: a silver-framed miniature of his own mother, with two dark-haired little boys gazing up at her.

There was an envelope with *Miss Randolph* inscribed on it, but the envelope was empty. He sharpened a quill to try again, and took her little yellow rose out of his pocket for inspiration. Words just did not come. He had no right to say what was in his heart. Finally he picked up the carved sandalwood box filled with medals Robb had removed from his uniform, to make Darius less a target. He put that on top of the empty envelope. Then he stared at the fire until it was time to wake Robb and Hugh.

"What are we doing up so early?" Hugh asked as he staggered into the morning room, wiping his eyes. "We don't have to be at the Oaks for hours."

"Breakfast, my boy, breakfast."

Hugh's face took on a greenish cast when he saw the mounds of food on Conover's plate. The night's revelries hadn't set well with him, nor did the idea of facing his sister if things did not go the way she wished. "How can you eat at a time like this?"

"Easiest thing in the world," the major answered around a nearly raw beefsteak. "You better get used to it. A soldier has to eat when there's food. You never know when the next opportunity will come. Right, Robb?"

"Yes, sir. Many's the time we had naught but what were in our pockets, and no way of knowing how long it had to last. 'Sides, no sense in dying on an empty stomach." Having served the major, Robb was standing by the sideboard, picking out his own breakfast of kippers and cutlets.

Hugh's coloring turned even more bilious.

"At least have some coffee, Lieutenant. Settle your nerves."

When Hugh was seated, trying to avoid the sight of all that food, he noticed the dog. "What's old Fitz doing here? I thought he always went home when the company left."

Darius shrugged. "He wouldn't leave. And let me tell you, if the condemned man got one last wish for company, it wouldn't be Fitz. He snores."

Reminded of the duel, Hugh swallowed hard and said, "Don't joke."

Robb just shook his head. Young cawker's tender sensibilities wouldn't last long at the front. He poured out an ale for Major Conover.

"Uh, Major," Hugh asked, "you going out in your uniform? I mean, shouldn't you be wearing black or something?"

"Black is for funerals, Randolph. If the French didn't manage to kill me all these years despite my being as easy to spot as a peacock in the snow, then I'll just take my chances with Berke. I can't think he'll have trouble seeing me at twenty paces, no matter what I wear. Robb did remove the medals over my heart, if that makes you feel better."

Hugh noted how the uniform jacket was a tight fit over Conover's broad chest, now that he'd regained his weight and perhaps a little extra. Hugh eyed the major's plate again. "Maybe you'd do better to remove the coat anyway, free your arm up better."

Darius continued cutting his steak and chewing. "Mm. I'll think about it, if it's warm enough."

Hugh nodded, but was still troubled. "Some of the, uh, gentlemen last night were a bit above par."

Robb snorted. "Castaway, more like."

"I saw no reason not to open my brother's cellars, Hugh. If I'm around, I'll replace the bottles. If not, Cousin Preston doesn't deserve that fine old brandy half as much as my fellow officers. At least they stood by me."

"Zeus, didn't mean to find fault with your hospitality, sir! No, it's just that some of the men's tongues were loosened a bit—in their cups, don't you know—and, well, m'sister's name was mentioned more than once in connection with the duel."

Darius put his fork down, forcibly. "Your sister is not involved in the duel. Her name is blameless, and don't you let anyone convince you otherwise. Next thing we know, you'll be issuing challenges like Berke, and making Sonia's name a byword for real. The talk will die down after today, you'll see, so don't do anything harebrained. Do you understand, Lieutenant?"

When the major used that tone of voice, Hugh did. "Then the whole thing really is about a game of cards?"

"Don't be a nodcock. I wouldn't give the time of day to Berke or Preston. Do you think I'd sit down to a hand with them? I walked into the room, saw the two of them, and left. The whole thing was a farrago of nonsense."

Hugh was skeptical. "Then why? Mean to say, a

fellow hates you, so he avoids you. No need to start a brouhaha. That's why everyone's looking for deeper reasons. Couldn't still be that old rapper about Berke's sister. As you say, he's got nothing to gain by shaking the skeletons out of his own closet."

Darius swirled the liquid around in his glass. "I don't know about that. I might be wrong, and there's no way to prove I'm right, but I think Berke has a lot to gain. You do know he's nearly always below hatches from gaming?"

"Everyone knows that. He's at the clubs every night."

"As long as you realize he's a basket-scrambler and don't let him near your sister."

"Sunny? She's too downy a bird for that! She tolerates him for Lady Atterbury's sake, but just barely."

"Good. Anyway, I had my man do some checking to see where Berke gets his income. It's not from his lands; he bled them dry years ago. They are mortgaged to the hilt. And he's not even a particularly successful gambler. Yet he always seems to come about, at least enough to maintain his standing on the town. My cousin Preston, on the other hand, has more money from his mother's family than he knows what to do with, and keeps winning more."

Hugh digested that. "You mean Preston is backing Berke?"

"Something like that, and Preston could be calling in his markers. As I say, I could be wrong and Preston could be supporting his wife's brother out of the goodness of his heart. Then again, pigs could fly. I cannot think of anyone else who will benefit by my demise."

"Lud, why didn't you ever say so?"

"What for? It's just conjecture. Milo always stood between me and the title, and I thought I'd die a hero anyway. Much better than taking one of

Berke's bullets over some lightskirt. He always was a crack shot, you know. That's why it was so easy for him to make the challenge. He never believed he could lose. I thought at the time that if I met him and lost, that would be half confessing I knew the girl."

"Uh, are you any good with a gun?" Hugh thought to ask, a trifle late.

Darius smiled. "Passable." He reached for another rasher of ham.

Hugh was still mulling over the information. He was not a quick thinker at the best of times, but before dawn was especially taxing. "Still don't figure about the girl, Berke's sister."

"According to Berke, who I'd trust as far as I could throw, she named me. But what if she said Conover? I know I never laid with her. She was a bran-faced chit with rabbity teeth. Fellow'd remember a thing like that. Preston's a Conover, too; Conare's just a jumped-up title he bought from Prinny. Maybe that's why he's been settling Berke's accounts for all these years."

"And Berke couldn't force him to marry the chit because Preston was already married. Gads, his own sister-in-law!"

"Maybe Berke didn't know or didn't have proof. Or else he was trying to protect his other sister, Rosellen. Maybe he even thought to blackmail Preston. It's possible we'll never know. Once he challenged me and slandered my name, he couldn't back down without looking the fool." He shrugged. "It's all idle speculation now at any rate. At least it will be over soon." He tucked a scrap of yellow silk back into his pocket from where it had lain next to his plate. Then he got up and began filling another dish.

Hugh had to hold a napkin to his mouth. "Lud, you're not going to eat all that, too, are you?"

Darius answered, "No, it's time to leave," as he

selected lamb chops and a sirloin with the bone left in, potatoes and gravy, a muffin or two.

Halfway out the door, Hugh complained, "Well, if you ain't going to have another meal, what in the blazes is that?"

Darius put the plate down on the floor, under Fitz's nose, and smiled as the dog started gobbling. "Insurance."

I wasn't ready.

Chapter Nineteen

*T*hat's it! That's how man, truly just one of us higher species, manages to maintain his domination. No, not by his fancy fingers or use of tools, nor by his convoluted thinking, by Tray! Canis Major, it's pockets!

He can store things. Oh, squirrels bury nuts, and dogs hide their bones, and foxes take food back to their dens all the time, but I mean really store things. Man doesn't have to be worrying about his next meal, so he can keep larger issues in mind. He can even keep two things in mind at once.

While some of us are only recently come to the security of steady meals, human persons have long since gone beyond the drama of mere day-to-day survival (except the very poor, of course, but no one seems to count them). Men have transcended immediacy.

I saw food. I ate it, like my fathers the wolves, like my cousins the jackals. An atavism, that's what I am. I am as stupid as the squirrel who can be tempted into the open with a handful of corn. Squirrel stew. That's me, squirrel stew.

The only times man allows his appetites to overrule his reason are when he's in his cups, or in the act of love. Cat dirt, I should have got him foxed! I could have found him a woman. One waits at the corner every night. No, those would only have been temporary solutions. The major was not likely to forget his purpose, not like me, I am ashamed to admit.

My dreams of being inscribed in the annals of canine glory have been written on the wind. I was going to be a hero, like Aubrey's dog, Dragon, who not only identified the Frenchman who slew his master, but took the varlet on in single combat before the king—and won. I was going to equal Dragon in valor. They would have named a star after me.

Dragon, hah! My full belly is dragging, that's all. My tail between my legs, I go home. Miss Sonia will need me. My place is by her side.

"Well, you picked a fine time to stay out all night," Sonia complained to the dog who drooped next to her chair. "I'm awake all night worrying, and you're out tomcatting! A nice how-do-you-do." The dog looked up at her from under shaggy gold eyebrows, whimpered once, and went back to sleep. Sonia went back to polishing silverware. Technically this was Marston's job, cleaning the fragile heirloom epergnes and candelabra. The butler had grown lax and fumble-fingered; Grandmother should see about pensioning the old fellow off. Sonia didn't mind the chore anyway. It gave her something to do, and the polishing table in the butler's pantry was right beside the front door.

Here it was after ten and she'd received no word. She gave a tiny swan-shaped salt cellar a hard buffing. Her brother had sworn to come to her as soon as there was word. She wanted to throttle him. She nearly rubbed the wings off the poor swan instead. Next she attacked a monstrosity of a centerpiece, with elephants marching around the base, trunk to tail, howdahs on their backs, palm trees overhead, monkeys in the trees, and large, parroty-type birds on top whose open mouths were candle holders. Even Lady Atterbury hated it. The thing was a wedding gift from Great-Aunt Sophrina, so it stayed. Today it was getting the polishing of its life. The palm trees were almost swaying.

Where was that chaw-bacon brother of hers anyway? she fumed, rubbing an elephant until it squeaked. Everyone knew duels were at dawn. If he'd stopped off at the barracks, she'd— What if he was busy with surgeons and things? Darius had said trust him. She did, of course. But she didn't trust Ansel Berke, or the accuracy of dueling pistols, or the skill of some unknown physician. She didn't even trust her heart to keep beating through all this waiting. What would she do if— No, she was not going to think about that. Just let him live, she prayed, even if he flees to America or back to the army. That's all she was asking, for now.

By eleven the monkeys on the centerpiece were screaming for mercy, and Sonia was starting on the parrots. Ian had taken Fitz out and was dragging the reluctant dog up and down the street in front of Atterbury House, watching for the first glimpse of Lieutenant Randolph. The dowager was out of her bedchamber for the first time in days, running Bigelow and Sonia's maid ragged with her demands for possets and potions. Marston stood erect by the front door, magnificent in livery and powdered wig. Only the glazed look in his eye revealed that the dignified butler was as drunk as a lord. Sonia polished.

"He's coming!" Ian finally shouted from the corner, to be echoed a moment later by Marston's stately "Lieutenant Randolph approaches," as he marched across the marbled hall to report to the dowager in the drawing room. Sonia jumped up, sending polishing cloths and powders every which way.

"He's alone!" Ian called.

"The lieutenant appears to be unaccompanied," Marston intoned, crossing the hall again. Sonia clutched the centerpiece to her chest, sending a monkey or two hurtling through the palm trees.

"He's whistling!"

Marston silently slid down the wall to land prostrate on the marble. The centerpiece soon joined him on the floor. Sonia jumped over both to run down the outside stairs and throw herself into Hugh's arms, dirty hands and soiled apron and all, right there on the street.

"Tell me, tell me!" she cried, tugging him back up to the door. "Who won?"

Hugh jingled some coins in his pocket and whistled again. "Why, I did, don't you know. Laid m'last month's pay on the major. Got good odds for Conover's bum leg and Berke's reputation."

"Dash it, Hugh, you know I don't care about your addlepated wagers! What happened?"

Hugh got a glimpse of his grandmother fanning herself in the drawing room, so he pulled back. "Uh, what say we go to the dining room, have a bite to eat, what? Didn't get much of a breakfast, by George."

"You'll get in here this instant, young man, and stop your confounded shilly-shallying," Lady Atterbury demanded. "Warebourne survives, I assume?"

Hugh bowed and nodded.

"And Berke?"

"Him, too," Hugh replied, looking pleadingly at his sister.

Now that she was not on tenterhooks, Sonia could take pity on Hugh. If she couldn't save him from their grandmother's rancor, at least she could feed him. She sent Bigelow and Maisie off to see about a substantial tea for her brother, since ringing for

Marston was going to be useless for some time to come.

Hugh didn't speak while the servants scurried back and forth with trays and platters. He did mention, though, around a thick slab of fresh bread with a chunk of cheese on it, that he hadn't stayed for the postcontest festivities at the Golden Hare. "That's why I'm so sharp-set. Knew you'd be anxious, so I rode back straightaway."

"And Darius, Major Conover, is at the Golden Hare? *Celebrating?*" Sonia asked. He was off enjoying himself while she was in such agony?

"Devil a bit," Hugh answered, making himself another sandwich with some cold meat. "He's on his way to pick up the Warebourne chits in Lyme. Said the coaches were all packed and ready, and he missed the brats. Wanted them near him, he said. Can't imagine why, m'self." He kept eating.

Sonia tossed a napkin at him. "But what happened? You still haven't told us about the duel!"

"Oh, that. Neatest bit of shooting I've ever seen. Quickest golden boys I ever made." Lady Atterbury angrily drummed her fingers on the armrest of her chair. "Uh, better to start at the beginning."

"Finally," the dowager muttered.

Hugh ignored her, preferring his sister's eager smile. "'Twas foggy. Usually is for this type of thing, early morning, don't you know. Trees look spooky." Lady Atterbury cleared her throat; Hugh rushed on. "Anyway, we were there first. Darius wanted to be early so his men could scour the woods to make sure no sharpshooters were hidden in the trees."

"He never thought Ansel Berke would be so dastardly!" the dowager insisted. "The man's a baron and a prime marksman, from all I hear."

Hugh shrugged. "Darius is a soldier. Said it pays to be careful. His man Robb says the major hasn't led his men into an ambush since he was a green 'un on his first foray out. Besides, that Warebourne title might be worth something to someone else other than Berke."

"Conare," Sonia breathed, her hand to her mouth.

The dowager merely went, "Harumph. Jackanapes doesn't know what he's talking about. Gentlemen like Berke and Conare do not behave like savages. Proceed, sirrah."

"Well, Conare didn't show his face anyway. Berke came along in good time with a parcel of mincing fops, all their high-heeled slippers getting stuck in the grass. At least Berke wore Hessians. He was laughing and carrying on with the coxcombs as if he didn't have a care in the world, comparing snuffboxes of all things! Let me tell you, such confidence drove his odds down."

Hugh sat up straighter with self-importance. "I conferred with his man. He conferred with Berke. I conferred with Conover. Neither man would apologize."

The dowager snorted. "If they were going to apologize, you looby, they needn't have waited six years!"

Affronted, Hugh told her, "My job, don't you know, trying to negotiate a compromise."

"Hush, Grandmama, let Hugh tell the story his own way."

Hugh nodded toward his sister. "Right. We loaded the pistols. Have to admit m'hand wasn't quite steady, all those old fa—fops watching. Then we marked off the paces. The baron and Darius took their places. Berke was all in black, once he buttoned his coat and turned up his collar. Darius stood in his shirt-sleeves. Some old court-card rattled out the call. They paced. They turned. And Darius shot the pistol right out of Berke's hand before the baron even lowered his weapon to fire it!"

Sonia clapped, and Her Grace let out her breath.

"Right. Darius must have been practicing, the way he swiveled on that good leg of his. I've never seen the like. And his shot destroyed one of Manton's prettiest sets. One's no good for dueling, you know. Have to be a matched pair. Well, Berke started crying foul. No one listened, and they were his crowd, all congratulating the major on a deuced fine shot. So Berke screamed louder that Darius fired early. The old gent who was judge looked down his long nose at Berke and declared it a fair fight. Made the baron look a fool, with his hand getting all swollen and red from powder burn. He drove off in a snit."

"And then?"

"Then cool as you please, the major and Robb whip some jugs out of the carriage and set 'em up for target shooting. Sure enough, the sheriff and the magistrate come not five minutes after Berke left. And what do they see? A bunch of gents taking practice. Nothing havey-cavey about that, though some of the shooters were a bit on the go. I won another bundle from the magistrate, betting on Darius. None of the others would take him on, naturally. Anyway, as soon as he could without giving offense, the major sent 'em all off to the Golden Hare, breakfast on him, while he and Robb drove off. I got to bring the curricle home."

"Will the baron be satisfied, do you think?"

"He'll never challenge Darius again, that's for sure. And you can bet none of those other chaps will think to insult the major either, not after the exhibit he put on. My guess is they'll laugh at Berke if he tries to stir up another mare's nest."

"Honor was satisfied," the dowager declared. "Berke knows better than to destroy his own credibility."

"Thank goodness," Sonia said, pouring her brother another cup of coffee, then fussing with the sugar tongs. "And did the major, uh, say when he was coming back?"

"No, but he told me to pass on that he'd call as soon as he returned." Hugh grinned. "And he did ask for Papa's direction. Thought he might stop off in Berkshire on the way. Too bad I had to tell him that the governor is halfway to Scotland. My last letter said Father expected to wait nine months for a grandson, and nine months it would be."

"That inconsiderate imbecile!" Her Grace's displeasure rattled the teacups.

"Darius?"

"The major?"

"No, you blitherers, Elvin Randolph! Disporting himself with a young bride when for once in his life he should be at home with his stinking sheep! Here's a catch for his daughter, and he'll let it slip through our fingers with his cavorting. Yes, cavorting like a cockerel!"

Hugh grinned again. "Somehow I don't think Sunny's bird is going to fly the coop so fast."

"Nothing's been said," she protested, to which Lady Atterbury snorted. Sonia could feel the heat rising in her cheeks, but that only matched the glow in her heart. He was going to speak to Papa. Sooner or later. Then she recalled her grandmother's words. "Does that mean you approve, Your Grace?"

The dowager raised her lorgnette to her nose and stared at Sonia. "I have always liked the boy," she lied. "It was his situation I deplored. Now he is on his way to being a respected member of society, a hero, an earl with at least fifty thousand a year. Have your wits gone begging, girl? Of course I approve."

That afternoon a bouquet of flowers was delivered for Miss Sonia Randolph, eighteen yellow roses. The enclosed card read *Yrs., Warebourne*. Not very loverlike, but considering the interested audience of Lady Atterbury and her cronies, Blanche, and Hugh, Sonia silently thanked him for sparing her further blushes. She was especially grateful when they all felt the flowers and the card required some comment.

"Very proper," one of the old ladies decreed. Another added: "Just the right touch."

Lady Atterbury nodded. "The boy has class. I like that."

Blanche just said, "Very nice." She was patently disappointed the major hadn't made any protestations of undying love. So was Sonia, but she kept that to herself, along with the relevance of the yellow roses.

Only Hugh voiced his discontent. "He signed it Warebourne. Sounds like he's selling out."

"What did you think, you clunch?" Lady Atterbury asked. "He was going to fetch the children so he could take them with him to a war? Or did you suppose he was going to call on your father to buy some hounds so the officers could have a hunt in Portugal? No Harkness granddaughter is going to go following the drum, not while I live and breathe. You really are woolly-headed, Hugh Randolph. Your father should be proud."

"I wouldn't mind traveling with the army, Grandmama," Sonia said, thinking of Blanche and Hugh, and also that she didn't want Darius to give up his career for her.

"No one's asked you, missy."

As a matter of fact, the thought occurred to Sonia—and to everyone else—that no one had asked her anything.

Human beings think too much.

Chapter Twenty

Cogito, ergo sum. I think, therefore I am. Of course you are! What did you suppose, you were the worst nightmare of a herd of beef cattle? Or did you rationalize that since a rock cannot think, a rock does not exist? Descartes should have stuck to mathematics!

Sometimes men are all thought and no action. They dillydally when they should just do it! Now Darius found another impediment not to get on with what Tippy calls "a marriage of true minds." He cannot find Miss Sonia's father! That's true mouse droppings! He thinks, therefore I am at a loss.

What if the first bud of infatuation fades? What if it never blossoms, but withers on the vine? That happens. There has been no offer; there is no ring. Nothing to make crying off a major social disaster. For barking out loud, there is nothing to cry off *from*, except some sighs and longing looks. The pigeons who hang around Almack's for the stale refreshments no one eats say there's many a slip twixt the cup and the lip. In Berkshire we say, don't count your chickens until they hatch. What if all this comes to is an omelette? Those pigeons, the fattest I've ever seen, are full of stories of fickle females and rakish gentlemen who seem to fix their interest, then move on.

And there is adultery, the ultimate in fickleness. Miss Sonia was raised better, but what of the major? I understand that couples often spend this infinity of indecision, then the year's betrothal, go through with saying their vows before man, God, and the licensing bureaus—and break those same sacred vows as easily as eggs for breakfast. If Darius Conover thinks to throw Miss Sonia over, or be unfaithful to her later, better Berke had shot him, by Pluto!

I can't think. I'm too busy worrying.

A single yellow rose was delivered to Atterbury House at three in the afternoon for the next ten days. Sonia kept the roses in a vase beside her bed, then pressed them in her Bible. She kept the notes, which all read *Yrs., Warebourne*, in a drawer with her gloves and handkerchiefs. On the eleventh day, the rose was delivered late, not until dinner, and in a small gold filigree holder with a brooch back. All the previous flowers had been wrapped in tissue with a ribbon, all of which reposed in yet another drawer. The eleventh rose had no note, but was obviously to be worn, and tonight was Wednesday. Everyone knew what that meant.

Sonia spent the next hour selecting a gown to wear to Almack's. She finally settled on an ivory satin that had gold lace trimming at the hem and around the neckline. Sonia had never worn the gown, considering the décolletage too immodest for her taste. Madame Celeste had insisted the dress was much less risqué than that worn by most debutantes, and that Mademoiselle had the figure for it. Bigelow agreed with Sonia that the deep vee was suggestive—"Muslin company"—and suggested Miss Randolph tuck a lace fichu into the neckline: "Some lights are better hidden under a bushel." Sonia thought the filmy lace took away from the gown's classic lines, so she never wore Celeste's creation. Tonight the ivory satin was perfect, with the yellow rose nestled between her breasts. There was no lace fichu.

Lady Atterbury bestirred herself to attend the Marriage Mart that evening, wearing her favorite purple taffeta, with diamonds on her chest and an egg-sized ruby in her turban. Hugh was commandeered as escort.

"What, for stale bread and lemonade? Or the chicken stakes in the card room?"

"Neither. You come to lend your sister countenance."

Hugh grinned. "She'd do better if you lent her a shawl." He tempered his teasing with an affectionate hug, telling Sonia she was in prime twig.

Darius was already in the King Street assembly rooms. He was at Sonia's side before she greeted the hostesses, cutting through the horde of admirers clamoring around her. He signed her card for the opening cotillion and one other set, late in the evening. There was no chance to speak, with Monty Pimford reciting his latest masterpiece and Wolversham requesting a dance so he could explain Coke's newest theory. Darius most likely could not have spoken anyway. He knew how impolite it was not to look a person in the face when addressing him, or her, but he couldn't lift his eyes from Sonia's soft, lush, velvety—rose, he told himself. Look at the rose. No, look at her eyes. He gave up and moved away before embarrassing himself completely.

Sonia followed him with her gaze, as did many another female, both young and old. Darius had chosen to make his first invited entry into the bastion of the haut monde also his first appearance as the Earl of Warebourne. He wore the satin knee smalls that were de rigueur, and the black satin evening coat established as the mode for gentlemen. His waistcoat was white marcella with subtle gold thread embroidery, and his neckcloth was conservative, except for the yellow topaz and diamond stickpin. All in all, he was clothed befitting an earl, and his clothes fitted to perfection. His soldier's build, all hard muscle and broad shoulder, was almost as noticeable in Weston's handiwork as in one of Lord Elgin's Grecian warrior-athletes. Sonia's eyes hardly left him as she absentmindedly conversed with her other acquaintances.

When the music finally started, Sally Jersey was reluctant to part with the most elegant, virile man at Almack's that night. She had no choice. Before she could lay a dainty hand on his sleeve to restrain him, Lord Warebourne was gone.

He bowed to Lady Atterbury, then held his hand out to Sonia, not trusting that his voice wouldn't crack like a boy's. Sonia was nearly as tongue-tied at his magnificence, wondering if such a handsome, sophisticated nobleman could possibly be interested in plain Miss Randolph, now that he had the world and its daughters to choose from. She was too practiced in the social graces, however, to stand mumchance fretting. She knew a lady was supposed to initiate conversation when silence threatened, so she thanked him for all the lovely roses.

Darius swallowed. "I, ah, see you are wearing my token." See? He could hardly look elsewhere or remember whether he was doing the Roger de Cleavage or the bosomlanger. Luckily the dance was a cotillion, so he did not have to change partners.

Sonia smiled. "Of course I am wearing it. You sent it. But tell me, my lord, why eighteen that first day?"

Now he looked directly into her bluebell eyes, which were at about the level of his chin. Just right.

"You are eight and ten years old, your brother said. A rose for each precious year."

"I should have known you'd be even more smooth-tongued as an earl, my lord," Sonia replied with a dimpled grin, pleased beyond measure at his words.

"What, are you about to start 'my-lording' me like everyone else? I won't have it."

"Still giving orders?" she teased. "You shall have to decide which it's to be, my lord earl or major, sir."

"Darius."

"Darius," Sonia repeated, winning a warm smile. "Then I do not have to be stuffy Miss Randolph?"

"I have never met anyone less stuffy. And I think you have been Sunny to me since I heard your brother say it. Even before, but I didn't know the word. Do you mind?"

"Of course not, silly."

"Of course not, *Darius*," he corrected, just so he could see her dimples flash again. "But that's only in private, you realize. For now." At her raised eyebrows, he went on: "You do know I have tried to contact your father? I have sent letters to every inn your brother George mentioned, and half the great houses of Scotland. It appears your esteemed parent wishes to remain undisturbed on his wedding trip. Blast him!"

Sonia giggled, delighted at his evident frustration.

"Minx. Until I have word from your father, I intend to see that not one hint of impropriety touches your name. None of the old tabbies will utter the slightest meow of disapproval."

"But I do not care what they say. I've never been a prunes-and-prisms miss, you know."

"I know it well, and am thankful you're not a pattern card of decorum, else you'd never have given me the time of day. And I never cared what they said about me either. Nevertheless, I find that

179

now I care very much that no blame attaches itself to you from my attentions."

"What, not even one step over the line?" She looked down at the rose at her breast. His eyes followed, as she knew they would.

Darius painfully dragged his gaze to her soft, smiling lips and even teeth, her little pink tongue. "Unprincipled baggage! Not even a smidgen of gossip, so don't tempt me. By Jupiter, if I wasn't determined to do this up proper, do you think I'd be satisfied with two miserly dances? Especially when I know every ramshackle rake in the place will be looking where he's got no business. Let me warn you, my girl, I do not intend to be any complacent . . ."

"Complacent what, my lord?"

"Darius." He bit his tongue. For once in his life he was going to do everything by the book, even if it killed him. If ever he needed to throw something . . . "Just understand that I would ask for every dance, if I could."

"And I would answer yes," Sonia told him, without subterfuge or coy flirtatiousness. Which caused Darius to forget all of his resolutions and raise her hand to his lips, which caused them to miss a step, which caused the couple behind to bump into them, which— So much for resolutions.

Everyone at Almack's that night knew it was a match, even without Lady Atterbury's not so carefully veiled remarks about Elvin Randolph's unfortunate absence. By tacit consent, no one mentioned the old scandal, especially after Blanche let slip a clue or two about Hermione Berke and Preston Conare. Having heard Hugh's suspicions, Blanche decided this was the best plot she'd come upon, surely too delicious not to share, particularly if it could smooth her friend's path. Blanche took extra pleasure in mentioning to that haughty Lady Rosellen that no one held *Darius* Conover to blame. Rosellen ignored Blanche, but then she always did.

Rosellen was too busy to listen to platter-faced

chits and their empty prattle. Like many another lady there, she was trying to attract the man of the hour. Rosellen unobtrusively pulled at the already plunging neckline of her favorite red satin before moving to stand by Lady Atterbury's chair when Darius brought the troublesome Miss Randolph back. The chit was supposed to be Ansel's meal ticket. The dangerous new earl was supposed to be fair game to an enterprising female.

"Ah, the prodigal son is returned," Rosellen quipped when Warebourne bowed in her direction after Sonia tripped off with some green boy. "And they are serving up the fatted calf," she suggested evilly.

Darius merely raised his eyebrows.

"Of course, some men don't like sweet new wine with their meals," Rosellen went on. "They prefer a riper vintage, tart and spicy."

"Some older wines turn vinegary," Darius commented.

Watching from her place in the set, Sonia was making note to inform Lord Warebourne that she, Sonia Randolph, did not intend to be any complacent whatever either! Then she saw Rosellen scowl and stomp off. Darius winked at Sonia as if he felt her pique from across the room and was telling her there was no need for concern. She would have felt better if she'd heard what sent Rosellen off in an angry swirl of draperies: "And some men don't care for mutton dressed as lamb."

Whoever at Almack's did not know of the unofficial engagement was quickly apprised when Darius claimed Sonia's hand for the first waltz. All of his nobler aims flew by the board when Sonia simply walked into his arms and said, "I've been waiting forever for this." Darius recalled, a bit too late for his expressed objectives, that Miss Randolph did usually get her way.

* * *

There were other opportunities to dance in the next days, although never enough. They held hands in the shadows at the opera, stayed touching a moment more than necessary when Darius helped Sonia on with her cloak, or up to his curricle for a ride in the park. Where his instincts may have overridden his better intentions, Lady Atterbury's resolve held firm.

"One premature infant in the family is enough," she commanded, rapping his fingers with her lorgnette after they'd lingered overlong on Sonia's waist. Sonia laughed to see the stalwart hero reduced to blushing schoolboy, but she, too, started wishing that her father might grow a little homesick for his lands and dogs, if not his children and new grandson.

The dowager was so intent on keeping decorum—and a good twelve inches—between Sonia and the earl that she exerted herself to attend many evening functions she'd previously considered too fatiguing. How tiring could it be to boast of her granddaughters, one already a marchioness and finally breeding, the other soon to be a countess? Even rackety Hugh seemed to be headed in the right direction, which was wherever Lady Blanche and her title and acreage led him. Unfortunately the featherheaded chit was fixed on following the drum; Lady Almeria thanked her lucky stars she did not have the keeping of that hen-wit.

During the daytime, while the dowager conserved her strength, she still made sure Sonia was adequately chaperoned. Hugh and Blanche went along on every outing, with Sonia's maid, her groom, Ian, and even the impossible mongrel. Lady Atterbury was further reassured when Warebourne brought his man, his nieces, and their new nursemaid. Miss Inwood was a responsible, respectable young miss sent by the children's grandmother to replace the flirtatious Meg Bint. Lady Atterbury would have rested easier if the entire British blockade were along to play dogsberry for her granddaughter and that devilishly handsome lord, but what could happen on a jaunt to Richmond with so many in the party?

What could and did happen was that Ian, always one to appreciate a pretty face, took Miss Inwood and the children off to explore the maze. Hugh and Blanche strolled through the gardens lost in a discussion of military maneuvers, and Sonia's maid, Maisie, was pleased to share her picnic blanket with the major's man, Robb, behind a yew hedge and out of sight. For all intents and purposes, Darius and Sonia were alone on a wool throw, except for one large black dog who insisted on more than his fair share of the blanket. Fitz's usurping sprawl naturally forced the blanket's other two occupants into closer proximity. Neither Darius nor Sonia complained.

As anyone with a ha'penny's worth of sense could have foreseen, Sonia was soon wrapped in Darius's arms, half in his lap, half out of her gown, fully out of breath.

A kingdom may have been lost for a nail, but an ant crawling across Conover's neck saved the day. "No," he vowed, as he returned to his senses. "No." He set Sonia away from him. "And fix your gown," he ordered. "And your hair, and . . . and do something about your mouth. For pity's sake, not that!" he groaned, when she ran her tongue over swollen lips. Sonia gurgled with laughter to see him drag his fingers through his own tumbled locks. She reached out to brush a curl off his forehead, but he firmly pushed her hand away. "None of that, minx, or I am lost. We'll talk."

Sonia thought he was just about the most enchanting sight she'd ever seen, spouting propriety and giving orders with his cravat all rumpled. She kissed his nose and quickly sat back. "Very well, sir. What shall we talk about?"

Darius leaned back on his elbows and smiled. "I spoke to some of the younger party members. They think I can make a difference in Parliament if I take my seat. There are crucial votes for military spending and such coming up."

"Then you won't mind being an earl?"

He looked around: blue skies, flowers, laughing children, and sweet Sonia instead of mud and muck and blood and horror. He laughed out loud. "If this is a taste of civilian life, I'm all for it! There are others in the army who can do my job just as well, and I think I can be of importance to the War Office here. Treatment of veterans, conditions for the enlisted men, just expediting supply deliveries. There is much work to do."

"And you can help support the bills protecting climbing boys and limiting the hours for children in factories and mines."

"Gads, Sonia, you expect a lot. I know nothing about such measures."

"But I do," she told him with perfect complacence.

"Very well, with your help I can certainly do more for climbing boys and child workers while in Parliament than I could while in Spain. And I have to see about Ware, too. I've been leaving everything to the stewards and estate managers, but I'll have to make some decisions soon, although the devil knows how. I know even less about farming than I do about legislature."

"But I know more. Especially if there are sheep. And Papa will be ecstatic to help; he's worse than Lord Wolversham when it comes to new methods and improved production."

"Will he like me, do you think?"

"Go grouse hunting with him once and he'll adore you, for your aim alone. And if you admire his hounds, his sheep, and perhaps his new wife, Leah, he'll welcome you with open arms. Mostly he'll love you when he sees how happy you make me. You are happy, too, Darius, aren't you? You truly don't mind selling out?"

He had to squeeze her, just once for reassurance. "I doubt I'd make a good officer any longer, Sunny. My heart and mind would be back here with you and the girls."

"And boys."

He grinned. "Sons, too. What more could a fellow ask?" He leaned back again. "I must be the luckiest man alive! Look up. That's how I feel, that I could reach up and touch the sky. No clouds, just sunshine. Sunny and me. There is nothing I cannot do, or be, thanks to you. Everything is perfect!"

"No, Darius. You are perfect."

He reached out and touched her cheek. "If you believe I'm perfect, then I am."

The Greeks had a word for this. They called it *hubris*.

Chapter Twenty-one

𝒯 he Greeks did not think this hubris, this pride and self-confidence, was such a good idea. Then again, the Greeks didn't think much of dogs, either.

There's an old story—I know, not another dog story! What did you expect, Puss in Boots?—of Alcibiades, an Athenian statesman and soldier and regular rum touch, if you ask me. One day he went on a tear, rampaging through the city during his wild revels. Then he went out and bought a dog, the prettiest, most expensive greyhound he could buy, for suchamany drachmas. And he cut off the dog's tail. For Spot's sake, he did! When asked why, Alcibiades answered that he did it so the Athenians would remember *that*, rather than his earlier wanton destruction. They didn't. In fact, aside from Plutarch and us dogs, no one remembers the tail at all. Nor, when they hear of Alcibiades, do they recall that he was a famous general or a student of Socrates'. No, what comes to mind first about Alcibiades is best expressed in the schoolboy's taunt: Ace likes lace. The Greeks didn't think much of women either. No wonder their civilization did not last!

Anyway, so much for pride. The Greeks believed that the gods took retribution on men who rose above their station. Things are not so personal anymore. Nowadays people just say, Don't tempt fate, or Knock on wood. Would lifting my leg on a tree do as well?

The major should succeed at politics. I heard no overweening determination to reach the top of government positions, no burning desire to run the country. I agree with the Great Republican: Greed and ambition are not particularly desirable traits in those who hold office. The major had none of those tendencies. Maybe now I can relax.

"Your father, my dear, is a very elusive gentleman. Does he never answer his mail?"

Sonia's cheeks pinkened to match her jaconet walking dress. Her grandmother's sentiments had not been quite as delicately phrased.

"That Elvin Randolph should be strung up by his thumbs," Her Grace declared. "Why, we're the bobbing blocks of the ton. They're all speculating he's been without a woman so long since your mother died that he needs must make up for lost ground. Balderdash! I know all about his convenients in the village, and so I'll tell anyone who asks. We will not even be able to have a fashionable announcement ball if that nodcock stays away much longer. Everyone will be off to Bath or their country properties, hang him."

"He promised George to return for the baby's christening next month, Grandmama, and you know I never wished for a big squeeze anyway."

"Gammon. We've waited this long for Itchy Britches Elvin, we'll not have any hole-in-corner affair. Do you hear me, miss? I finally got my butler sober."

Sonia just nodded and smiled. She was going to let Lady Atterbury throw London's grandest bash for the engagement because Her Grace's heart was so set on it, and because the dowager had put up with so much already. Then, however, Sonia was going to have the wedding of *her* dreams. She'd be married in the Sheltonford chapel, with Vicar Gilcroft officiating, just as he'd officiated nearly every Sunday of her life. All her friends, neighbors, tenants, and staff would come to see her father give her away. Blanche could be maid of honor, and Fitz would wear a bow. Vicar Gilcroft simply had to let Fitz in the church, just this once, without it being the annual blessing of the beasts; there'd have been no wedding, no meeting at all, without Fitz. Sonia also planned on three little flower girls strewing rose petals and orange blossoms. After the wedding they could all go to Ware for the summer instead of on an extended bridal journey. Sonia was anxious to start meeting her new tenants, helping to care for the lands.

Miss Randolph kept busy meantime, but not too busy for her old friends or her little friends. She and Fitz often met the Warebourne girls in Grosvenor Square after their visit with the admiral. Sonia made sure the girls took part in her other activities when possible, like excursions back to Richmond Park or events like an evening at Astley's Amphitheater. She often accompanied the trio on simple outings to Hyde Park to feed the ducks. Fitz learned to leave them alone—the ducks and the bread.

One day Sonia arranged to keep the children company in the park while Darius kept an appointment with the War Office. He was working on getting Hugh transferred to his own cavalry regiment, where, he told Sonia, his former comrades would look after the lad. Hugh would not be made a fool or cannon fodder, and the colonel's wife was sure to take Blanche under her wing if the war dragged on. Leaving Sonia with her servants and the girls, Darius promised his nieces ices at Gunther's later; his eyes promised Sonia at least a stolen kiss or two when he returned to fetch them.

Sonia and the children had a wonderful time, training Fitz to be a circus horse, like the performers at Astley's. They'd brought a hoop along to play with, and taught Fitz—and Baby—to jump through.

Genessa said she was practicing for teaching her new pony, when they returned to Ware for the summer. Benice thought she'd make her kitten a lace tutu, for her to wear when she rode the pony or Fitz.

"I think we shall have to ask the cat, my dear," Sonia told her, "and the pony."

Gen tried to wrest the stuffed dog from Baby's hands, to ride atop Fitz with a hair ribbon as reins. Bettina protested, loudly, so the new nanny, Miss Inwood, sent the older girls off a ways with the hoop, while she held the toddler and the toy on her lap. Bettina was not reconciled.

"Here," Sonia volunteered. "Give me Tiny, Miss Inwood. I haven't had a coze yet today with Mimi."

Sonia looked up from the baby's prattle a few moments later when the older girls stopped their chatter and gathered closer to her skirts. Sonia raised her head and looked around to see what had caught the children's attention, Preston and Rosellen Conover promenading toward them. Sonia stood, still holding Tina, and curtsied. "Come, children, make your bows to your cousins."

Benice made a stiff curtsy and whispered, "Lady Conare, my lord." Gen made the slightest bobble, and the baby threw herself back into Sonia's arms.

"Still as unmannerly as ever, I see," Lord Conare derided, taking out his quizzing glass.

Bettina hid her face in Sonia's shoulder. Sonia almost wished for a big shoulder to lean on herself.

Instead she spoke brightly: "We've been having a lovely day, haven't we, girls? Do you want to show your cousins what you've been teaching Fitz?" Tina clung harder, Gen shook her head no. Even Benice, who could usually be counted on to do the pretty, scuffed her toe in the ground.

"My dear Miss Randolph," Conare drawled, "as sweetly charming as I recall. And foolish. What makes you think we'd possibly enjoy seeing children and dogs frolic about? Why aren't the brats in the classroom anyway? Surely they could be learning something other than how to become common performers."

Miss Inwood was starting to bristle at the slur to her charges and her competence. Sonia intervened. "Why, Miss Inwood has done amazingly well in no time at all. Genessa knows her letters and numbers, don't you, precious? And Benice is halfway through an exquisite sampler. I'd be surprised if she does not become a notable needlewoman, with such patience and dexterity." Sonia chuckled. "Much more than I ever had as a child. They have come along so well, in fact, that we declared this perfect spring day a holiday."

Sonia's effort won a shy smile from Benice, but a sneer from Conare. "I had assumed my nieces were not learning to be sheepherders." He raised his quizzing glass from the now-quaking Benice and fastened his enlarged eyeball on Sonia. "And 'we'? I have not heard any interesting announcement. Perhaps I missed something to account for your inexplicable interference in my young cousins' education."

Rosellen snickered. "And as for patience, the on-dit is that you and Warebourne have none. Be careful, my dear, for nothing is so hard to hook as a fish that's already stolen the bait."

Sonia looked worriedly to the children while Conare added in that affectedly slow voice of his: "I am not sure Milo's children need to learn quite that much of the world at their tender ages."

Miss Inwood put her arms on the older girls' shoulders, and Ian took a step closer to his mistress. Sonia counted to ten before she started to wrap her tongue around a few choice words to blister the supercilious pair's ears. Before she began, however, Fitz ran through his new paces. He jumped through the hoop, which was held loosely in Gen's hands. The hoop got away, rolling across the damp grass, onto the dirt path, and over Lord Conare's shiny Hessians. Preston jumped back, sending the hoop in Rosellen's direction, where it left a muddy ring right across the hemline flounce of her sheer peach-colored muslin.

"Why, you little brat!" she screeched at Gen. "You did that on purpose. I've a good mind to—"

No one found out what, because Rosellen was positively not in mind to confront the large growling dog that stood between her and her intended victim. Rosellen grabbed Preston's sleeve and demanded he escort her home immediately, before anyone noticed her begrimed skirts.

"Cousin Rosellen is a wicked, wicked witch," Gen declared when the pair was out of sight. Sonia did not bother rebuking her. Shaken, she hugged the baby with one hand and smoothed back the dog's bristled ruff with the other. Benice's lip trembled, and Ian and Maisie looked ready to charge after the disappearing couple, so Sonia gathered her composure and said, "Well, we shan't let unpleasant people ruin our pleasant day, relatives or no. I believe I have just the thing in my reticule, a wonderful story of knights and ladies and dragons." She straightened the baby's dark curls, which reminded her of Darius's. "And a lot of pictures. Here, Miss Inwood, you take Tina and I'll find the book."

When Sonia handed over the child, however, Maisie Holbrook exclaimed, "Oh, miss, your silk spencer is all wet. The babe must have drooled all over it."

"Oh dear, I cannot go to Gunther's looking like I'd been under a spigot, and I promised the children a story. I know. Maisie, please return to Atterbury House and fetch my blue spencer. It will match the trim on my gown equally as well as this damp one."

"Of course, Miss Randolph. I'll just hop out of the park and hire a hackney at the gate. I'll be back before the cat can lick her ear."

"Fustian, Ian and the coach are sitting right there doing nothing. He'll drive you."

"Pardon, ma'am, but we couldn't both go off and leave you alone here."

"Nonsense, Maisie. I will not be alone with three children, a nurse, and a dog. Besides, you'll make better time if you don't have to walk to the park gate. At any rate, no one can protect me from insults, which is the worst one can expect in Hyde Park in the afternoon."

An unwanted and unexpected proposal was worse.

Ansel Berke had his driver halt the coach near Sonia's bench. He strolled closer while Sonia was reading the picture book. Fitz sniffed stiff-legged at the baron, who swatted at the dog with his walking stick. Fitz growled and went to investigate the crested, closed carriage.

"A word with you, my dear?" the baron oozed, striking a pose before her bench.

Sonia had not seen Berke for the last sennight or so. He looked more pasty-faced, less polished somehow. His clothes were all the stare, just a trifle awry, as if he'd dressed in haste. Sonia could not judge the condition of his gun hand, not with his gloves on. Injured or not, the baron was not her choice of companion. Even his heavy cologne nagged at the back of her throat. "I am sorry, my lord, but as you can see, I am occupied right now.

Perhaps if you call at Lady Atterbury's in the morning—"

"No, no, just a moment of your time," he urged, rudely pulling the book out of Sonia's hands and thrusting it at Miss Inwood. "The nanny can read. Do come, just a step, my dear."

Sonia did not want the children or Miss Inwood to hear anything else not meant for innocent ears, so she did get up. She walked a few paces away, not toward his carriage, but back along the carriage path, still in sight of Miss Inwood and the girls.

"Do hurry, Lord Berke. I am expecting Dar—Lord Warebourne shortly." She said nothing else, but the baron's color rose.

"Ah yes, Warebourne. That is precisely what I wished to speak of, my dear Miss Randolph. Word has reached my ears that there is a possible understanding—"

"Lord Berke, please do not say another word."

"I must! Please believe I have your interests at heart. You cannot know that scoundrel. Why, my own sister—"

"My lord, I insist you cease this conversation at once. I can only find it distressing and distasteful." She turned back to the children, only to find the baron in her way, on his knees.

"I beg you, my dear, marry me instead. I'd make a far, far better husband. No unsavory past, no sniveling dependents, and I have always been one of your staunchest admirers. You must admit my regard is long-standing."

"I . . . I am honored by your offer, my lord. However, I am already committed to Lord Warebourne, in my heart if not in the record books."

Berke got up and brushed at his knees, frowning. "And I cannot convince you to change your mind, albeit the dastard will play you false?"

"No, my lord. If Darius Conover should walk past right now"—Sonia only wished—"with a demirep on one arm and your sister Rosellen on the other, I would not marry you."

Berke left her in the path. "So be it."

Sonia rejoined the children as his carriage drove off. She shook her head. What an odd afternoon it was!

"Do you wish to finish the story?" Miss Inwood asked.

"No, you continue. I think Fitz and I shall walk back along the path to meet Ian and Maisie. The sooner I am out of this damp garment, the better I'll feel."

Sonia had no intention of going far, just far enough to get the stench of Berke's perfume out of her nose. Around a bend in the path, Fitz flushed a duck, to the surprise of all three of them. The duck quacked, the dog barked, and Sonia laughed as Fitz tore off after the flying fowl. Sonia whistled for him. "Come on back, you clunch-head. You've never caught so much as a fly."

The dog lumbered back, tongue lolling happily as he crashed through the underbrush along the walkway. When his noise abated, Sonia said, "Oh dear, I think I hear Tina crying. We'd better go back." Then she heard Genessa yell, Benice squeal. She started running. "Go, Fitz," she shouted to the dog, sending him ahead faster than she could move in her narrow skirts. "Go see, Fitz, go." Fitz passed her in a black flash, barking.

The dog never heard the thud of a walking stick hitting the back of Sonia's head, nor her scream as a blanket was thrown over her.

Only half-aware from the blow, Sonia struggled as hard as she could when she felt herself being lifted and shoved onto a cushioned seat. A door slammed and a familiar voice called: "Drive on, Jeppers, but not so fast as to arouse suspicion."

"You'll never get away with this," Sonia gasped through the blanket's folds.

"Why not? Who's going to tell, the dog? By the

time they find you, you'll be committed to me, in deed, my dear, if nothing else. I think I'll enjoy that part. And all the money, of course, when you have to marry me."

"Never," Sonia vowed as she slipped into unconsciousness, the cloying scent of Berke's cologne the last memory she had.

Never have I regretted my mixed blood more.

Chapter Twenty-two

Bon chien chasse de race. Breeding tells.
Miss Sonia was behind me when I sped to the
children. Nurse was on the ground, moaning.
Baby was shrieking and turning purple. Gen
was screaming, and even quiet Benice was sobbing and trembling, staring at the blood on
Miss Inwood's temple. I dashed back to see
what was keeping Miss Sonia. Help! I barked.
Help! Hurry! Only she was not there. One whiff
of the carriage trundling down the roadway
told the story: My mistress was kidnapped.

Great Dog Star, what was I to do? My mother's blood raced through my veins with every
quickened beat of my heart. The chase, the
chase! View Halloo and never let go! Never lose
the quarry, even if your heart bursts in your
chest. My nose had the scent. My eyes had the
sight. My feet itched to be off.

But my father's spirit also suffused my mind.
Stand and defend the innocent. Protect the
vulnerable, the valuable. Stay with the lambs

you were given to guard, no matter that keeping them from harm means giving up your life.

I ran back to the crying, frightened children. Nurse was still on the grass. I ran forward to the path. The coach was rounding a bend. I ran back; I ran forth. There was no answer. So I did the only thing I could do. Tossing aside generations of breeding, I reached inside to my visceral ancestors. I sat down, threw my head back, and howled. Aw-woo. Aw-woo.

"What in the blazes is that ungodly noise?" Darius asked Robb, seated beside him in the curricle. "It sounds like all the hounds of hell are baying at the moon at once."

Hugh called over from where he rode his chestnut alongside the carriage: "Get used to it. That's m'father's favorite sound. In fact, reminds me of his old hound Belle. No other dog ever had a voice like that except—"

"Gads, Fitz!"

Curricle and horse raced down the carriageway, sending strollers fleeing like ninepins.

Ian and Maisie were returning with the Atterbury vehicle at the same time, from the opposite direction. They had, in fact, passed Berke's coach.

They all met in the clearing near the bench and poured onto the greensward, leaving the blowing horses for Robb to tie. Maisie quickly took charge of Miss Inwood, holding her own apron to a bleeding head wound while Ian half carried the nursemaid to the carriage.

Darius knelt by the nearly hysterical children, gathering them all close as he tried to soothe them and find out what happened. Hugh stood by helplessly while Fitz kept up a continuous keening howl.

"Dash it, Hugh, at least get Sonia to shut up the blasted dog!" Hugh looked around at the same moment it occurred to Darius that Sonia was missing.

"Hell and damnation!" Darius tried harder to make sense of the children's garbled tale of circus tricks and runaway hoops.

"Please hush, Gen. Whatever happened could not possibly be your fault. Benice, sweetheart, I am counting on you to be your own levelheaded, sensible self and tell me where Sunny went."

Benice didn't know. Between sobs that turned to hiccups under her uncle's steady confidence, she managed to tell him how Miss Sonia went for a walk, that way, after a man talked to her, some time after Cousin Preston and Lady Rosellen were in the park. "And they said awful things to Sunny, and Fitz growled at them, so they left. Then the other man came."

"Did you know the other man, Benice?"

"I think it was the same mean man we saw at Miss Sonia's house the day we brought Fitz there. Miss Sunny went off with him and got mad. We could tell. But he went away, and Miss Inwood was reading. Then another man came, a bigger man I never saw before, and hit Miss Inwood and then ran into the bushes. We screamed and Gen tried to kick him, but he got away. We yelled and Fitz came, but not Sunny." She started to weep again.

"Don't worry, Benice, we'll find her. And you were very brave, Gen. Now, do you remember anything at all about the man who hit Miss Inwood?"

"No, but the first man had a walking stick. He tried to hit Fitz with it."

"And he had a waistcoat with big green dragonflies on it."

"And he smelled funny."

Darius cursed under his breath. "Berke. It has to be him, and his henchman or such."

"I'll kill him," Hugh swore, but Darius answered first: "You won't find enough pieces of him left." Then he became the complete army officer, organizing his campaign, deploying his troops, giving his orders.

"Ian, you take Maisie, Miss Inwood, and the children to Ware House. The staff can look after Nurse and send for a doctor if needed. Gen, Benice, I am counting on you to be brave and look out for Tina for me so I can go after Sunny."

"I want to go with you, Uncle Darius."

"I know, Gen, but I need you to guard the home front. Do you understand? Robb, you go with Ian to Ware House and get my pistols. Saddle up and go—Deuce take it, I don't know where!" He ran his hands through his hair. "Hugh, where is Berke's country place? We could go haring off in every direction and lose each other *and* the trail."

"I think his seat is in Oxfordshire, but that's crazy. Surely he'll go north to Gretna, so we just have to follow the pike."

"That's if he means to marry her."

Hugh started cursing, softly, for the children's sake.

"No," Darius thought out loud. "He must want to wed her, but she will not be willing. Now, there's an understatement if I know Sonia. He'll have a battle on his hands the whole way to Scotland, so I bet he'll just get her out of town, into a rented lodging or a wayside inn, and keep her there until she agrees."

"That miserable—"

"Yes, but there are a lot of roads out of London, and a lot of inns. We'll have to figure he took his own coach, at least, so he wouldn't need strangers along for the abduction. Someone's bound to remember seeing the markings."

The dog's howling had turned to yelps as Fitz dashed to and fro along the carriageway. Darius studied his movements. "We'll start this way, out of the park. Fitz seems sure. At the gate, you go north, Hugh, in case I am wrong and he is headed for Gretna Green after all. You can go faster on horseback. I'll follow Fitz. Whoever picks up a trail sends a messenger back to Ware House for Ian and Robb. Make sure you leave messages along the way, and I'll do the same. Robb, if you haven't heard from either of us by dusk, go to the Runners. Ian, wait as long as you can before alerting Lady Atterbury."

When the others nodded their agreement, Darius sent the carriage off and watched Hugh use his heels on the chestnut. He climbed into the curricle. Fitz jumped up beside him, whining.

"Yes, I know, old boy. We'll never let her out of our sight again. Now, hang on, Fitz, you're in for the ride of your life."

Sonia awoke to a fierce headache and the rumbling of a carriage. The blanket was on her lap, thank goodness, no longer over her head. Her hands and her legs were tied, and the window shades were drawn on the carriage. Ansel Berke was seated across from her in the gloom with a smug smile on his powdered face, so either she was having the most detailed nightmare of her life, or the pompous ass really was abducting her for her dowry. After he stole her virtue.

She tested the bonds on her wrists under cover of the blanket. The carriage was traveling slowly enough that she could hope to survive a jump from the coach if she could only get her hands free. Sonia thought they must still be in the city, from the lack of speed and the traffic noises she heard, so she ought to be able to find help, once on the street. With the curtains drawn, she had no way of discerning direction or destination. She just knew the sooner she was away from this bedlamite, the better. Unfortunately, although the bonds were not painfully tight, she could not undo the knots.

Sonia decided to try reasoning with the baron again. She did not bother appealing to his sense of honor, justice, or fair play. Sonia never spent her coin on lost causes. Berke had already proved his dearth of scruples by the kidnapping, so her only hope lay in convincing the thatch-gallows that his scheme was doomed to failure.

"It won't work, you know," she told him. "No matter what you do, I'll never be your wife. I'll refuse to make the vows."

"As I said, you'll have no choice, my dear. Your family will insist on the marriage."

"My family will accept my decision no matter what happens."

He cackled. "You truly are an innocent. Lady Atterbury will welcome a leper to Grosvenor Square before a ruined woman. Unless I open them, every door will be closed to you."

"Not my father's," Sonia insisted.

"From what I hear, he doesn't remember *having* a daughter. Do you really think his new young wife wants a tarnished spinster under her roof? I knew Jennifer Corwith during her season. Grasping chit, her dowry was too paltry to put up with her puling. Nevertheless, your brother's wife ain't about to want scandal touching her new position, precarious as it is, with the squire taking her own neglected stepsister to wife. As for your sister in Bath, why, Backhurst is as proud as he can stare. He most likely won't let Catherine even correspond with a fallen woman."

Sonia set her mouth in a determined scowl, especially after she was forced to acknowledge the truth of his arguments, so far. "George's wife and Catherine's husband might place public opinion above family. My papa never will. He'll take care of me, so you'll never get a groat of my portion."

Berke leaned toward her and laughed again, an unpleasant, humorless sound. Even his breath was foul, unconcealed by his stagnating scent. "Your papa will take care of you?" he sniped. "The way he took care of you all your life, letting you run wild about the countryside? Oh yes, my dear, I know all about you and your delightful family. You suit me to a cow's thumb, you see, so I made the effort. The ton is already half-convinced you are no better than you should be. A night or two at a posting house should turn the tide."

"I repeat, never."

No longer amused at her resistance, Berke leaned back on the seat opposite hers. "Your opposition is gallant, my dear, and I do appreciate not being treated to tears and the vapors. However, you waste your breath. You'll marry me if I have to find a Newgate friar. If I have to drug you or knock you senseless. Your consent is not required, Miss Randolph, so save your strength for tonight."

Now, Squire Randolph may have held a loose rein over his youngest daughter, but he never sent her unprotected on her rambles. He made sure she had her dog—and a dirty trick or two. He taught her to use reason first, but when that failed, foul play. Sonia felt she'd tried being reasonable, without getting through to Berke's self-interest, if nothing else. Now she brought her hobbled legs up to seat level and kicked her booted feet forward, right where they were certain to get the baron's undivided attention.

"This way, eh, Fitz?" Darius was regretting Robb's absence. Every time he wanted to get down from the curricle to seek information, he had to find an urchin or an ostler to hold the fractious bays. His leg was starting to ache, and his mood was growing blacker and blacker as the traffic moved slower and slower. His only consolation was knowing that Berke was making no better time through the congested streets. Some blasted victory celebration, Darius cursed.

When they did come to a halt behind a water wagon or whatever, or when they reached a crossroads, Fitz leaped down and sniffed around as often as the major. The dog whined and circled, then jumped back up, barking. Soon Darius took to watching the dog as much as the horses and the other vehicles. Fitz seemed to know what he was doing, and the major's instincts told him to follow the animal. Those same instincts had kept Darius alive for years, so he aimed his cattle where the mongrel's nose pointed.

"I hope you're right, old boy, but I don't know how you can be so sure. They have a good lead on us. Do you think you can find Berke's coach in this mess, huh, Fitz?"

Of course I can. I peed on it, didn't I?

Chapter Twenty-three

$\mathcal{S}$ome wag once said that fleas are good for a dog. They keep him from brooding about being a dog. Dogs don't brood. Hens brood. Do you know how little it takes to make a dog happy? A full belly, a soft bed, a kind word are usually enough. Why should we brood?

It's not dogs who are unhappy with their lot. We're not the ones who always want more than we have, more than we need. It's man who is top dog at greed.

Like the baron. Talk about brooding! He should have had so many fleas, he'd have time for nothing but scratching. That might have kept him from wanting more and more and my mistress! He had a title and a tidy competence. They were not enough. Gambling did not increase his wealth, so he tried to steal Miss Sonia's portion, especially, I think, because she was to be Conover's mate. Greed.

Napoleon is greedy. He gambles with whole armies and he kidnaps entire countries. Do complete nations of men share their avarice?

No, that's foolish beyond belief, even for such flea-brains.

Besides, I have to pay more attention now.

The streets are crowded. Many carriages, horses, and pedestrians have passed this way. The noise of a military band a few blocks over saturates my senses, so it is harder to concentrate. Still, I know we are on the right course. If only we could hurry some.

Then the major went off the scent, no matter how I told him different. He told me to hush, that he's cutting through back alleys and side streets to gain back some of Berke's lead. If the baron was on the road ahead, which I knew he was, we might come out ahead of him. A fine military maneuver, if successful. Otherwise we could be dodging through narrow lanes and cluttered alleys, chasing our own tails.

I was ready to jump down. I could make better time on my own, ducking between carriages. Then we intersected the main road at a corner where a sweep was working. The major tossed a coin to a peg-legged man in a tattered uniform. "Can you hold the horses, soldier?" he asked.

The veteran took a bite of the coin in his hand and vowed he'd treat 'em like high-priced whores. Now, *that* should make Caesar and Jupiter relax. I yipped at them as I dashed past. They'd stay put.

Other horses and their drivers cursed at me as I ran between hooves, under carriage beds, circling. Was Berke still ahead of us, getting away, or was he just coming toward the intersection? A night-soil collector had just gone by. I couldn't smell a thing!

The major was standing up on the curricle seat—good thing I told those nags to stand still—looking in both directions. "There he is!" he shouted, vaulting down and running ahead. I was right at his side.

The major stopped by the sweep, threw another coin, and snatched up the lad's broom. The man has gone queer as Dick's hatband, I thought. I ran ahead, closing in. Then the broom sailed over my head, javelin-style. All that practice paid off. The broom finally slowed and flipped end over end, right in front of a crested coach-and-four. Those were four horses who suddenly believed in sorcery. They started bucking and rearing in the traces, looking for the witch and screaming about being turned into Americans or something. The driver had all he could do to keep them from bolting through a dress shop window. Soon every horse on the street was making noise and mayhem, horses being as excitable and subject to suggestion as adolescent girls. The drivers were shouting, nothing was moving on the street. People were pouring out of stores and a corner tavern.

We ran in for the kill. The major pulled the carriage door open, reached inside, dragged Ansel Berke out by his collar. I was his comrade in arms. I was brave. I was brutal. I gave no quarter. My growls rolled across the street like the mighty lion's roar stretched across the great savannah, as I went for Berke's throat. . . .

"Get back, you overgrown dust mop, I knocked him out with the first punch." Darius threw the limp baron to the street like soiled laundry. Fitz immediately jumped onto Berke's chest, slavering into his face. Berke wasn't going anywhere. The major drew the rapier from his cane and brandished it for the sake of the driver. "Don't think of coming to his aid. Don't think of driving off."

"No, guv'nor. I ain't gonna think at all, if you say so. Never liked this job anyways. 'E promised me back wages if I went along, is all."

Darius wasn't listening. He was climbing back inside the carriage for Sonia. He used his sword to cut the bonds at her ankles and wrists, cursing the entire time. "Are you all right, Sonia? Did he hurt you? I'll kill him, by George, if he so much as touched a hair on your head."

When her hands were free, Sonia reached up to feel the back of her skull. She winced.

"He's dead. I don't care if I hang." Darius started to get out of the chaise, murder in his eyes.

"No, Darius. I am fine, truly. I do believe Ansel was coming to see the error of his ways anyway. He suffered much worse than I did, I assure you."

Darius took her in his arms then, right there in the closed carriage, telling Sonia that she was brave and clever, and Berke never stood a chance. His relieved outpourings were lovely, but Sonia began to fear her bones might break from his squeezing so hard. And the noise . . . She managed to loosen his grip enough to raise the curtain over the carriage window. A mob of people were standing around the coach, some angrily knocking on its side.

"Darius, please."

He released his hold on her, but only long enough to slip his arms under her legs and behind her back. He swung her out of the carriage. Some of the spectators applauded when he set Sonia on her feet.

"Coo, it's just loike a fairy tale, ain't it?" a young maid with a serving tray in her hand sighed. "Ain't 'e the 'andsome 'ero an' all."

Sonia winked at Darius and nodded her agreement to the girl.

A burly individual in a leather apron pushed his way to the front. " 'Ere, 'ere, wot's this about some toff runnin' off wit' a gentry mort? Oi'll give 'im a taste a home-brewed, oi will."

Another man in the circle guffawed. "An' that be just like you, you great lummox, t' come on like a bloody Crusader after the war be won. It's the dog wot has the skirter. There be naught for you t' do wit' yer great bloomin' muscles 'cept flex 'em for Polly 'ere."

Some of the other men laughed. The aproned fellow stepped forward angrily, but Darius held his hand up.

"Thank you all, good people," he said, "for coming to our aid. We still have need of your services to restore the lady." He pulled out his purse. "Might someone take a hackney to Ware House in Grosvenor Square to inform my household?"

Darius selected a messenger from the eager volunteers while the serving girl Polly blotted her eyes on a dingy apron. "A real nobleman, 'e be. I cain't wait t' tell me ma."

Darius passed a few more shillings around. "For your help in clearing the street and getting these wagons moving." Angry draymen cheered and returned to their carts and loads. Darius handed a coin to the girl with the tray. "Perhaps I can impose on you to provide some tea for the lady, Miss, ah, Polly? And you"—with a handful of guineas to the aproned bruiser—"if I am not mistaken, own that tavern yonder. Serve a round on me to everyone who has been inconvenienced." Another cheer went up.

"But wot about 'im?" one of the men asked, jerking his head toward where Berke still lay in the gutter, the dog on his chest snarling if Berke made the least move.

"Him?" Darius asked casually, snapping his fingers and whistling the dog away. "Why, he's mine. All mine."

Berke cringed, but maintained enough self-esteem—or stupidity—to get to his feet. He looked down on the muddy pawprints on his fawn breeches, the pulled threads on his dragonfly-embroidered waistcoat, the dog drool on his limpened neckcloth. He sat back down on the cobbles, all confidence and bravery gone together.

Darius was beyond caring whether he had a fair fight or not. Grabbing Berke by the frills of his shirtfront, he dragged the baron to his feet.

"Why, you bastard? Why have you done everything you could to ruin my life? What did I ever do to you?" A fist to Berke's middle punctuated the questions, but did not elicit any answers, so the major tried shaking the smaller man. "Tell me why, if you hope to live until tomorrow."

"L-l-love M-M-Miss R-Randolph," issued forth.

Darius did not like that answer. "You loved her enough to clobber her and kidnap her, and try to force her against her will? Whatever that is, it sure as Hades ain't love. You wanted her money. But you've been snapping at my heels before you ever set eyes on Miss Randolph and her dowry." He shook Berke again, harder. The sawdust calf pads sank to Berke's ankles. "For the last time, why?"

"M-m-my s-sister."

"Gammon. And still not good enough. You know I didn't touch the girl, just like you know I never cheated at cards." He gave another shake. Berke's corset snapped with a loud crack. Then the nipped-in waist of his superfine coat wasn't quite so nipped, buttons popping onto the street.

Berke groaned. "My other sister. Rosellen."

"Ah, finally something of interest." Darius allowed Berke's feet to touch the ground, but he kept hold of the baron's shirt. "Do go on."

"Rosellen wanted to be countess. She tried to bring Milo up to scratch, but he wouldn't have her. He chose Suzannah instead, but Rosellen never forgot. You were just a second son, a soldier, so she wed Preston. Then she found out about him and Hermione."

"So you did know all along."

Berke closed his eyes. "Rosellen couldn't expose her own husband without looking the fool. And she already hated the Warebournes."

"And you went along with her out of brotherly love?"

"Rosellen paid me. My debts."

"And when I came home from the war, she saw

her way clear to winning the title after all." Darius was revolted, not shocked.

"No, that was Preston's idea. He controls the purse strings."

"I'm surprised you dance to his tune. Seems to me you could have played the piper, with your lack of ethics."

Berke mumbled something Darius couldn't quite catch. Neither could the few spectators still standing around them on the side of the road. They moved closer. The tavern wench had fetched Sonia a chair, along with some lemonade, and stood next to it, mouth agape. "Coo, it's better'n a play at Drury Lane. Maybe 'e was too nice to blackmail the other gent. 'E looks too pretty to be so mean."

Sonia rubbed her chafed wrists. "I do not think he's too nice for anything!"

"Nor do I," Darius agreed. He took a firmer hold on Berke's collar. "Preston wanted the title, and Rosellen—well, her motives are best left unsaid. But yours? You were on the lookout for an heiress. Everyone knew that. You could have lined your pockets without challenging me. In fact, you could have sold your information to Milo, then me. I think there's more to this than you have mentioned."

"Preston . . . knew something about me." Berke licked his lips. He looked at Sonia, then away. "A youthful indiscretion, nothing more. But he threatened to go to the authorities, or the scandal sheets." He looked at Warebourne in desperation. "I'd have been thrown out of my clubs!"

Darius shook him one last time for satisfaction, then shoved him away. "So you were content to save your reputation by ruining mine. What was it, the usual hanging offense?"

Berke sank to the ground, staring blankly at his scuffed boots. He merely nodded, gulping back sobs.

"One more question." Darius spoke softly. "Milo and Suzannah's carriage accident?"

"I swear I know nothing about it," Berke babbled. "If Preston did, he never let on. There was no inquiry. But I didn't, I swear. I wouldn't. Please." He raised his hands in supplication.

"Zeus, you disgust me. The world would be a better place without you in it."

The baron's shoulders started shaking on their own. Darius turned his back on the sorry sight to greet Ian and Robb. The reinforcements had arrived, along with six servants in Ware House black and gold livery, on horseback, brandishing pistols.

"Good grief, man," Darius shouted at Robb. "You've armed the underfootmen! Can they shoot?"

"Nary a bit. The guns ain't loaded, except for mine, a course. You thinkin' I should aim it at this muckworm here?"

While Darius was still bemusedly observing his new recruits, Robb chuckled. "Right, sir. Gettin' 'em on horseback was the harder part. But I had to send two of the stable lads out for the lieutenant, and leave another couple of riders behind for carryin' messages. Someone responsible had to stay back with the young 'uns. This is what was left."

"Robb, you deserve a promotion. For now, though, I am afraid you and your troops will have to do escort duty. Baron Berke is leaving the country. You and your stalwarts will make sure he reaches his ship—any ship—safely. First, however, I believe yon innkeep will provide ink and paper. I am also certain Baron Berke will accommodate me by writing down his little tale. His passport, don't you know." He turned to the nobleman. "One-way passport. Is that understood?"

Berke moved his head up and down a fraction.

"But what about Preston and Rosellen?" Sonia wanted to know. "Those two blackhearts can't get away with all they've done to you!" Sonia was so angry, she looked as if she'd take on the miscreants herself.

"Oh, I think we can be forgiving of our cousins . . . from Jamaica. Preston has holdings there. He'll go."

Darius waved an arm at the ring of watchers. "He'll never dare show his face in London again."

" 'Ere, 'ere," echoed from the crowd. "Exile's too good for the likes o' him."

"Yer lettin' this 'un off easy, guv." The circle of spectators was growing larger again, and they did not want a peaceable ending at all. They wanted blood.

Darius was pleased to oblige. He picked the baron up once more, drew back a steel-driven fist, and completed Berke's disarrangement by repositioning the baron's nose. Then he lifted him bodily and tossed him into the coach. The mob cheered as the carriage drove off with Robb and Ian and its resplendent if reluctant mounted escort. Most of the onlookers dispersed, thinking the show was over.

Darius turned to Sonia, who had been applauding as loudly as the most eager street urchin. "Bloodthirsty wench, aren't you?" he asked.

"Oh no. If I were bloodthirsty, I'd have drawn his claret myself!"

"I bet you would have, my endless delight." Darius laughed out loud and opened his arms to her.

Sonia walked into his embrace like coming home. "I knew you'd come," she told him, ignoring Polly's smiles and the currently unemployed sweep's whistle.

"I'd come through the gates of hell for you, Sonia," Darius whispered in her ear, his hands caressing her back, sending thrills down her spine. "And I would not leave without you, for I'll never let you go again. I cannot wait on your father. I've tried to be patient and do things properly, but I simply don't have that kind of strength. Sonia, you are my sunshine and my heart's song. Please say you'll be mine, forever."

She looked up at him, straight into his soft brown eyes. "Darius, I have been yours, forever." Which required a kiss. The tavern girl wiped her eyes.

"Soon?" Sonia asked when the world stopped spinning.

"The banns or a special license?"

"Can we be remarried later, in Sheltonford chapel, with everyone there?"

"We can be remarried anywhere you want. Once a week. In front of the prince, Parliament, or the Pied Piper. Just soon!"

"Then we need a special license. The banns take three weeks, my lord earl."

"Countess Sonia." He tasted it on his lips, then on her lips. Polly was blubbering. Then Darius sprang back. "My God, Duchess Atterbury. She'll have me boiled in oil!"

Sonia laughed. "Don't tell me the hero of the hour is afraid of one old lady?"

He grinned back. "I'd rather face the Spanish Inquisition any day. But I'll do it, for you!"

This time the kiss lasted so long, the crossing sweep was making book with a knife sharpener, and the serving girl was sobbing.

"Here now, sir. Enough of that. You'll embarrass the lady." The peg-legged man led the horses and curricle over to them.

Darius stepped back. The sweep ran forward with the lord's sword-cane, and Polly retrieved the lady's bonnet. She wiped it tenderly with her tear-dampened apron before reverently handing it to Sonia.

"Quite right, soldier," Darius said while Sonia tied her bonnet's strings. "Thank you for reminding me of my, ah, duty. And the cattle look calm enough, too. The bays won't stand for just anybody. You must have a way with horses. Cavalry?"

"McConnell's Fifth, sir. Private Brown, sir."

"Brave lads, Brown. Talavera?" he asked, gesturing toward the veteran's missing leg.

"Right enough. And your own bum limb, sir?" the man queried back, recognizing a fellow military man.

"Salamanca." Darius looked around when he felt a tug on his sleeve. He couldn't misread Sunny's hopeful expression. "Seems to me—to us—that one of our finest shouldn't be out on the street like this. And I seem to need a groom. You're qualified, Private Brown, except one thing worries me."

Brown's face fell. "That's what they all say, sir. No one thinks I can do an honest day's work with my wooden leg." He turned to leave. Sonia was starting to sputter.

"No, both of you!" Darius stated. "I just worried that Private Brown might be offended if his duties included pony lessons for three little girls."

"Bless you, sir, I nursed enough Johnny Raws through maneuvers. Little girls and ponies'd be sheer heaven."

"Then climb aboard, man; we're off to find a special license. Here, darling, up you go."

Fitz jumped up between Sonia and Darius on the seat. They both gave him a pet before Darius gave the horses the office to start. "Good dog, Fitz."

Good dog, Fitz?

Chapter Twenty-four

$\mathcal{T}$hat's it? I win the day for them, save the children, sound the alarm, track the coach, subdue the villain. And "Good dog, Fitz" is my reward?

I suppose it's always been this way. Romulus did not name the city Lupa, though he and his twin Remus would be carrion without us. People are born under the sign of the ram, the bull, the crab, even the scorpion. No one is born under the sign of the spaniel, in the house of the harrier, on the cusp of the collie.

It's not just dogs, either, although of all the species, we give man the most love and loyalty. Does anyone remember the name of even one of Hannibal's elephants? Daniel gets all the credit for pulling the thorn out of the lion's paw. For barking out loud, Daniel was going to get eaten! No one congratulates the lion for his forbearance and sense of fair play. I could go on, but whining never brought dinner hour any closer.

And a pat on the head is enough, I suppose,

since I know my job was well done. So they won't name a star after me. I was very, very good. Thanks to me, we now have a house of our own, with tenants to help, villagers to visit, farmers to advise. We have laughter all the time: little-girl giggles and deep-throated rumbles and, yes, even the first gummy, droolly grins of Master Miles Cecil Randolph Conover, Baronet Ware.

Now I have more time to go visit the setter bitch at the game warden's cottage that I met a few months ago. There's one puppy in her new litter that I like to think resembles me. He's black, with my gold eyebrows, and his tail is cocked at just the right angle for a dog, jaunty yet dignified. There's something more about him. You'd recognize the right pup instantly. He's the one who won't stay in the whelping box, no matter that he falls on his nose climbing over the sides. He's the one who has to taste the straw and the grass and the morning dew. He chases sunbeams and growls at shadows. That's the one.

"Darling—"

"My love—" Darius laughed and tucked Sonia's hand back onto his arm. They continued walking on a slow tour of the nearby grounds, admiring the summer flowers. "You go first," he said.

Sonia listened to a bird calling in the woods. "I just wanted to discuss an idea I had about a school in the village, but it can wait. What did you wish to say?"

Darius groaned. "Only that you have to stop employing every waif and wanderer who passes by. The maids are already tripping over each other, and the horses won't have any hair left from all the currying they are getting from the excess of grooms we seem to employ."

"You cannot complain about the stables, my lord,

for you hired Brown yourself, and that half regiment he said needed positions. And you did agree that Polly was wasted at the tavern, especially since Maisie and Robb will be setting up their own household. And that poor girl whose family all died in the last influenza outbreak—"

Darius held up a hand in surrender. "But the others, Sunny. And the ones the vicar will mention to you tomorrow. I finally got Lady Atterbury to forgive me for marrying you out of hand. You know she said she'd have my liver and lights if we sent her any more untrained servants with sad stories."

"Oh pooh, that's just Grandmama. She was delighted with Portia Foggarty. Grandmama really did need a companion, and Portia's husband left her in dun territory when he went off to fight in Spain."

"Yes, but—"

Sonia patted his arm. "I know, darling. That's why I think we need a new school."

"We already have a school, Sunny. With two teachers, a maid, and a man-of-all-work. You are going to bankrupt even the Warebourne treasury, my pet."

"Fustian. We are increasing the holdings magnificently, and your investments are profitable beyond even your expectations. Remember, we went over all the accounts together just last week, so don't give me any Banbury tale of impending poverty."

He grinned and kissed her on the nose, where a sprinkle of freckles was starting to make a summer appearance. "You may hire as many unskilled workers as you wish, then, wife." He began to trail kisses down her neck.

Sonia was not to be diverted. "That's the point of the new school, Darius. The one we have is for children, to teach them their letters and such. I want another place where those adults in need can learn a skill. Weaving or fancy needlework, perhaps, or learning to keep accounts. Even cooking and the ways of polishing a gentleman's boots. Anything that might secure someone a position. Then they can earn their own way and need not depend on the parish rolls."

"Clever wife, saving me money in the long run. Have I told you lately that I love you?"

"Not since breakfast," she answered with dimples showing.

"Oh, much too long ago." He proceeded to show her in convincing fashion.

"And have I told you recently how happy you make me?" she asked.

"Never often enough. Come, let's go back to the house while the children are— What's that henwitted dog done now?"

"Fitz," Sonia ordered. "Put that puppy down! You know it's too young. I told you yesterday and the day before, too. I cannot imagine how the mother permits you to keep scooping it up and taking it away."

Darius knelt. Fitz gently placed the pup in his cupped hands.

"I don't know why Fitz persists in bringing us this same little fellow," Sonia said, stroking the shiny black fur while the puppy wrestled with his lordship's glove.

Darius grinned. "Don't you, my love?"

Now, don't get me wrong, I'm not ready to chase my last cat, but, after all, every dog must have his day.